PLEASURE HOUSE BALL

IRRESISTIBLE ARISTOCRATS
BOOK 3

SUZI LOVE

PLEASURE HOUSE BALL

Love revealed at a courtesan's ball.

Brenton, Lord Mallory, attends his first courtesan's ball in ten years to appease his concerned friends, though he'd rather stay home and read to his motherless daughters.

Though mortified that Brenton unmasks her at a scandalous ball, Lady Lillian Armstrong doesn't regret their night together.

But will the object of her girlish adoration still treat her as his best friend's little sister, or will he now see her as a mature and willing woman?

1 *820 Blackstone House*
    Twenty miles south of London.

Brenton, Earl Mallory, secreted himself behind a life-sized statue of a naked man and willed himself to stay as still as the statue shielding him so he remained invisible to those on the dance floor. Hidden from the two hundred guests spilling through the various rooms Lord Browning had opened for the Pleasure House Ball.

Clearly he'd suffered a moment of insanity when he'd yielded to his friend's emotional pleas to accompany him to this ball, because Brent had no intention of participating in the adventurous romps and or indulging in the hedonistic behavior that made these debauched balls famous amongst his British peers. Within a few hours, most of the attendees would be drunk on spiked punch and the illusion of sexual freedom, passed out on the floor, or claiming one of the dozens of upstairs bedchambers.

Michael, Viscount Laidley and Brent's distant cousin, may be the best friend any man could wish for but, like Brent's family, Michael fretted that Brent would never agree to reenter society. Hence Michael's determination to push Brent into attending this ball, despite him having little interest in watching a parade of ladies of the night select and seduce their next patron. Keeping a mistress was the last thing Brent was considering. If his often-expressed wish to be left in peace was respected by his friends or family, Brent would happily remain in seclusion at his estate and thus avoid mixing socially with his peers, the vast majority of whom had enjoyed sullying his wife's reputation and had ridiculed Brent's defense of Marion.

Four years ago, he'd lost all respect for a large portion of the upper echelons of London's society when spiteful gossip about his wife's affairs had shattered their marriage and destroyed Brent's taste for a hectic social life. Nothing had happened since to convince him that the morals of Britain's rich and titled had improved and he'd enjoy spending more time with them. If anything, the newspaper reports confirmed, each and every day, that London was a cesspool of rumors and that not one of those gossip-mongers cared a whit if their gossip was true or if their hatefulness drove people to drink and despair.

Michael's face appeared around the statue's well-endowed groin, and his cousin pointed at the marble man's appendage and laughed. 'Hoping the ladies will compare your equipment favorably to his if you stand beside him?'

Brent snorted. Although he'd dug in his heels and resisted Michael's efforts to encourage him to attend this ball, his cousin knew him well and could always tease Brent into seeing the humorous side of situations. With a nod of thanks, Brent accepted a glass of tepid champagne from his friend, took a sip, and choked. 'Damn it, Michael, I'll need something stronger than this horse piss if I'm to last longer than an hour in this chaos.'

Michael laughed. 'Drink up, my friend, because it's either warm bubbles or the house punch, which Browning will have laced with anything and everything he could beg, borrow, or steal.'

Brent shuddered. 'For God's sake, Michael, why are we wasting our time here? I've no intention of engaging a mistress and, if you really have your eye on one of the duke's daughters, you'll want to keep your distance from any of these...ladies.'

He waved towards the hundred or more females who continuously giggled and squealed, while prancing around the dance floor in a startlingly colorful display, as if their next meal was entirely dependent upon outshining every other female and being the first to catch the eye of a wealthy man. 'They're on the prowl for a rich protector and you, Laidley, are known to be one of the richest viscounts in Britain. And as your father's health deteriorates every week, you'll soon inherit his titles and estates. Making you an even juicier target.'

They studied the crowd in contemplative silence. Women, and girls, spent a fortune primping and preening for this ball. Both their working life and future survival relied on catching the eye of a gentleman and then encouraging him to open his fat purse and spend an obscene amount of money in support of a mistress.

'Michael, please may we leave? I've a superb brandy at my townhouse, aged for twenty years, and smuggled into the country at high cost.'

'Huh! You mean given to you, the local landowner, in exchange for turning a blind eye to the vast amount of smuggling that happens on your beaches.'

Brent shrugged. 'Little point trying to stop smuggling in Cornwall. They've been making their living that way for centuries. Besides, the wars are finally over and embargoes are being lifted. I'll soon be purchasing my brand legitimately.'

'Your local smugglers won't like losing one of their best customers.'

'I'm trying to convince them that they could earn a living in legal ways, but it's an uphill battle. Smuggling is in their blood, so it's hard to...' He sniffed, and sniffed again. Shook his head in denial. Ridiculous to imagine Lillian, his Lillian, was the wearer of that country orchard scent. Or to picture her here, at a pleasure house ball. Bloody hell, perhaps his family's worst fears had become a reality and he'd morphed from a recluse into a madman.

Brent's obsession with waterways and farming distressed his mother and sisters, because they believed, wrongly, that his idiosyncrasies indicated a slide into madness, especially after they'd discovered that he held lengthy discussions on sheep herding and field drainage with Lillian, his neighbor and lifelong friend.

Those conversations happened as he rode around his estate, alone, and while Lady Lillian Armstrong was living in London with her family. Her forced presence in the metropolis was a concession to her father, the duke, who didn't believe that any daughter of his should hide in the country while the scandalmongers, generally peers of lesser status than his own distinguished family, questioned whether Lillian was blameless over the betting and horse race that caused her husband's demise.

Even as children, Lillian had known more about land and farming than Brent had absorbed from the thick agricultural volumes his father had insisted he read. Though Brent wasn't so far lost to sanity that he expected an illusory Lillian to reply, talking through farm improvements with someone who understood the rainfall and flooding in this part of England helped him visualize drainage problems, and satisfied his need to discuss Cornwall with someone locally bred and who loved the area as much as Brent did. If Margaret, his quick witted daughter, had grasped the benefits of his one-sided conversations with Lillian, surely his family, as adults, could see how it helped farm planning and staved off loneliness. Margaret's constant chatter engaged Brent for a large slice of every day, but a child's chatter was a long way from having a satisfying adult conversation.

Now though, his olfactory senses were conjuring her up in person, or at least sniffing out some unknown woman who favored the citrus scents that surrounded Lillian like a cloud, and alerted everyone to her presence.

Michael stared at him and snorted. 'What on earth are you doing?' His friend looking amused, or perhaps bemused.

Brent shook his head again. 'Must be imagining things. I know only one person who wears that perfume and she mixes it herself, her own blend of citrus fruits. That woman is a lady and a duke's daughter and certainly wouldn't be attending a courtesan's ball.'

'Good God! You don't mean–' As Michael was the only family member Brent had allowed stay for more than two nights at his estate, Lillian was well known to him, and she'd once given Michael a tour of her greenhouse and her distilling room and shown him the ingredients for her citrus scent.

'Shush. Don't even mention her name in this licentious crowd.' He looked around but thankfully didn't glimpse anyone who might be the woman they whispered about. 'She's very protective of her private recipe. She wouldn't give it to anyone except one of her sisters. Perhaps one of them has escaped their parents and somehow ventured into this ball. If that's the case, Lillian will be furious when she finds out. As the older sister, she goes out of her way to protect the younger girls, though I've always likened that to locking the stable door after the horses have bolted. Her sisters... how shall I put it? They have a tendency to be behave in a reckless manner, no doubt because they often stayed with Lillian during her marriage. They had a ring side seat to every sordid thing that happened to Lillian at the hand of her husband. Geoffrey Armstrong, as we well know, wasn't a saint. Far from it. If even half the rumors we heard were true, Geoffrey took everything to dangerous extremes. Those ridiculous bets he was notorious for writing in the club betting books. Whoring in every bizarre brothel in London. Mark my words, Lillian's sisters will have had their eyes opened living in that household.'

Brenton swore under his breath. 'Damnation! You know what this means? I'm going to have to investigate that citrus scent. Find whoever is wearing a fragrance containing oranges and lemons. I'd like to pretend my senses were mistaken and I didn't suspect one of the duke's girls is here and chancing being exposed. Lillian will shoot me if I don't at least look, and perhaps stop whichever sister it is from falling into disgrace.'

Michael threw back his head and laughed. 'Sounds simple. Push your way through this crowd and sniff every lady you pass. Can't wait to see what happens after you've stirred up half the women, and men, in that drunken crowd.'

Brenton groaned. 'What else can I do? Lillian will think me an appalling friend if I don't search, especially if one of Lillian's sisters has arrived at Browning's without an invitation. Or been coerced into coming by some rogue who may threaten to expose her in return for favors. Or even worse, the lady might be mistaken for a courtesan. If one of Lillian's family members is in trouble, I duty bound to save her.'

'Ah, yes. Mallory the savior of women and their reputations, even Marion the cheat.'

'I'm going to look anyway. If I locate one of the girls, I must at least see that she leaves, immediately. Get her out of here unnoticed and return her home safely.'

'Which one could possibly be?' Michael peered out at dense crowd, as if willing one of the Mitchell sisters to rip off her mask and wave it above her head and give them a better chance to recognize her. 'Surely they've more sense than to venture into this debauchery, and I'd like to believe that no gentleman would bring an innocent lady here.'

'Candace is the most likely. She's next oldest after Lillian and has a very inquisitive mind. Always asking me difficult questions. Has reformist ideas on the way she, and all women, should be treated. But whichever sister it is, her presence at this ball is unacceptable. Whoever it is, she needs to leave immediately.'

'Yes.' Michael grimaced. 'The duke will explode if he hears that one of his precious girls is here. Heaven help any man who had the stupidity to escort one of them.'

'This crowd loves gossip more than champagne, so if Candace is recognized, word will spread faster than a grass fire in dry weather.'

Michael pointed to a group further down the sidelines of the dance floor. 'That's Lady Templeton in the orange mask and feathers and...I say, a very decadent damped down muslin gown. You know what that means? Melissa will have already wheeled out the names of any men or ladies with titles who are on the guest list from her weak-willed lover, Browning.'

'Weren't you her lover once?'

'Briefly. Never again. She eats green men for lunch.' He pointed at Melissa again. 'You watch. Any minute, she'll weave her evil way through the dancers and try to match people to names. Despite the different styles of gowns and enormous concealing masks, she'll work out who they are. She already knows many of the hundreds here so it won't take that snooping lady very long to ferret out anyone not in her circle of acquaintances. The woman is evil, and delights in spreading her amassed tidbits far and wide, wherever she can cause the most upset and create the most havoc.'

'Oh hell. That's all we need.'

Michael scowled. 'And I know from personal experience that she's not above blackmail when she's short of funds, which happens often when she's paying for a new lover. She likes them young and virile.'

'She tried to extort money from you? Why didn't you tell me?'

Michael shrugged. 'I was young and green and humiliated by my own ignorance.'

'Christ. Then meddling Melissa Templeton is the last person I want to bump into tonight. If she knows that I've left Margaret, and my estate, she'll run to my mother and sisters and say she's seen me at an acquiring ball. She's vicious enough to enjoy seeing me squirm if I'm forced to explain that you coerced me into coming. My family will assume I've finally abandoned my reclusive life, but only to take a mistress into my keeping.

'And for Melissa, truth or lies are all the same. She'll take revenge on any man who has refused her, which means you Brent.'

'I've not only rebuffed Melissa's blatant advances, but I've also refused to meet at least twenty of the ladies my family considers eligible to be my second wife. The constant nagging will start up again, and Melissa will be grinning like a Cheshire cat at my discomfort. I've fobbed my mother off for months by claiming I'm not ready to rejoin the social whirl, yet I'm here. At a damn courtesan's ball.' Brent groaned. 'My mother will hate me once meddling Melissa spreads her poisonous gossip She's done it before. Spread tales of Marion's infidelities, thinking it would make me want to jump into bed with Melissa. She was wrong.' He sighed. 'But that makes finding whichever Mitchell sister is wearing Lillian's citrus mix even more urgent.'

Brent stepped out from behind the statue. 'Come with me, Michael. I need your help. The orchestra is starting again. Can you weave your way through the couples going onto the dance floor. Pretend you're drunk and bump into the ladies.'

'Damn you, Brent, you're insane. Sniffing around ladies coming and going from the dance floor just isn't done. Their escorts are likely to take offense and give me a bloody nose. Besides which, I won't risk running into meddling Melissa.' He shuddered. 'Don't forget that I'll be in the same predicament as you if my family hears that I'm associating with ladies of the night, rather than being bored to tears dancing with one of the numerous tedious chits they throw in my path. My mater will complain and my pater will have no choice but to threaten to cut off my very-generous allowance.'

'If you think we've got a lot to lose,' Michael said with a snort, 'then picture the outcry if Candace is mixing with rakes and courtesans and meddling Melissa discovers her identity. Not even the duke's standing will protect Candace from the gossipmongers. She's to be presented next year with my sister, Fiona, so being here will ruin any chance she has of marrying well. And if it's known that friends of her family, you and I...' He stabbed a finger into Michael's chest for emphasis. "Knew a titled lady was present and we did nothing to remove her from danger, the duke will kick both our backsides. Publicly. And our families will be humiliated.' He groaned again. 'That sort of seedy story will tarnish Lillian's reputation, again, and stop her reentering society for another few years.'

'I thought you preferred having Lillian in the country, so you can see her more often.'

'I do enjoy her company, I must admit, but for her own sake she needs to mingle again in London next year, other wise she'll not meet any eligible gentlemen. Lillian is special. Too loving to avoid marrying again and becoming a mother. Bringing out her sister is the perfect opportunity to slide into the social events without creating too much of a stir.'

'Lillian's reentry into the social whirl will cause a stir, no matter what happens here tonight.'

Michael grimaced. 'That lowlife husband of hers did more than destroy his own life when he came off his horse. Racing through London's foggy streets at three in the morning proved what we all knew. The bastard died through sheer stupid arrogance. But if that wasn't enough to blacken the Armstrong name, someone started those preposterous rumors about Lillian goading him into the race.'

'I know, I know. Armstrong was so full of his own self-importance that no-one, especially his wife, could have talked him out of that race.' Brent ran his hands through his hair, forgetting that his valet had spent fifteen painful minutes combing his hair into the perfect style for a man about town. Personally, he couldn't give a damn about how he looked.

His normal style was casual and practical clothing, because his time was spent riding around his estate. Only if he was accompanying his daughter to visit neighbors would he don a coat and cravat, but for some reason his valet had decided that tonight he should look his best. No doubt one of his sisters had misconstrued his outing and instructed Henry to outfit him as a gentleman on the lookout for a wife. Laughable considering his first venture outside his estate was to a debauched ball, while he'd consistently told them he'd no intention of taking another wife, not yet anyway. His experience with marriage hadn't been pleasant, and after his wife's death he'd preferred to turn his attention to his young daughter, even if that meant becoming a recluse for the last four years.

So far, nothing and no one had changed his mind about a second marriage, despite hoping at some stage to give his precious daughter another mother. Margaret, the delight of his life, was better company than most adults, and the main reason he'd declined invitations to evening events around London, especially balls aimed at procuring a new mistress. Once his peers knew he was once again socializing, even if only at this lower level, word would spread that he was hunting for a bride. His peaceful Cornwall existence would be shattered by pushy matrons and unwilling chits. He shuddered.

Turning left, he eased into the crush around the edge of the ballroom, having pointed Michael in the other direction. If anyone knew his purpose, they'd certainly label him as a madman. Each time he passed a group of women, he slowed his steps and sniffed the air around them a couple of times, allowing their scent to fill his nostrils. So far, he hadn't detected any recognizable perfumes. Courtesans preferred heavier perfumes, scents that told prospective protectors that they were ready to negotiate the terms of a liaison, exchanging sexual favors for gifts of a house, servants, gowns, a carriage, and jewels.

Brenton passed another exaggeratedly-endowed marble statue, similar to the one behind which he and Michael had hidden. A stride or two beyond the six foot or more naked man, he stopped and sniffed. Inhaled again deeply. Orange, lemon, and a touch of bergamot, the aroma that always surrounded Lillian. A smell that reminded him of fresh air, sunshine, and simpler times. When they'd been children, they'd picked oranges straight from the trees on his estate, devouring them in the shade and later been berated by nurses and governesses when they'd returned home with stained clothing and sticky hands.

He sidled closer and stood on the dance floor side of the statue, where he wouldn't be seen but could peer from behind the exaggeratedly endowed naked man by tilting his head to the left a little. There were two women, both masked and wearing very low cut and rather sheer gowns. The woman dressed in red tugged at the bodice of her high-waisted gown, but to no avail. The skimpy strip of red fabric was barely wide enough to stretch across the woman's ample bosom and the tiny edging of lace refused to budge. Full-breasted ladies had always appealed to Brent, despite him marrying a lady whose breasts hadn't increased past a small handful even when swollen during pregnancy. A closer look was needed. He couldn't say for sure, but he thought Candace's breasts were smaller than this lady's. The thought of Candace slipping away from the safety of her home and mixing with these people dismayed him and would shock her father. However, the image of his sweet

Lillian entering this den of iniquity confused, bewildered, and terrified him.

He looked again, on one hand cursing masked balls because he couldn't see the faces and on the other, blessing those same masks for preserving anonymity. Lillian had large bosoms, so beautifully rounded that he'd often drawn on every ounce of willpower that he possessed to focus on her eyes when they spoke, rather than act the cad and drop his gaze to her magnificent chest.

He was no saint and he knew his limits. Knew he'd struggle to drag his gaze upwards if he even once viewed her incredible breasts at close range. Far better for his sanity and her modesty to admire the size and shape of her breasts at a respectable distance, and not risk doing something foolish. Schoolboys drooled when a maid bent to her work and inadvertently exposed the tops of milky-whole breasts, but Brent was well over thirty and hoped he was mature enough to have put his drooling days behind him. Though to be honest, if Lillian bent over and revealed her creamy flesh to his hungry eyes, he was likely to regress and gawk and gape like the gangly youth he'd once been.

Many years ago, he'd set himself strict limits with regards to Lillian and her sisters and he'd kept to his self-imposed rules. Other men stared at Lillian, and her beautiful sisters, though two of them were barely out of the schoolroom, but he'd always been drawn to women with substance and experience of the world, rather than blushing girls. Which, of course, was his present problem. Was one of these scantily clad women one of the ladies he knew? He had no definite proof, so he moved even closer to the two ladies.

Lillian was his best friend, plus a beautiful woman with a seductive feminine form and, right at this moment and in his direct line of sight, a pair of familiar bountiful breasts spilled over the top of a too-small red bodice. He blinked, and looked again. Heaven help him, it was Lillian. His friend who'd been targeted by unscrupulous women who, wanting to pull her down a peg or two, had blamed her for her husband's impetuous nature. A titled lady who, according to convention, should be secluded from society while she mourned her husband. Lillian, his Lillian, stood before him drawing the eye of every discerning gentleman at a courtesan's ball. Shock robbed him of breath and froze him in place. His head spun as he tried to imagine why she'd come here, and with whom.

As a duke's daughter, she'd been taught the rules for mourning and for the behavior of widows all her life. A minimum of six months wearing black and withdrawing from society, followed by another six months wearing mauve and lavender and socializing only with family and close friends. Brent could think of no reason why she'd be here, flaunting herself in that red slip of a gown. What had possessed her to attend a ball, any ball, so soon after her husband's demise?

More importantly, Brent's mind was so numb that he couldn't formulate a plan to hadn't smuggle her out and away from the dance floor before masks were removed and someone recognized her as the duke's daughter. Or before one of the lecherous men present realized that those were Lillian's breasts squeezing past them and through the crowded room.

First step was to uncover the identity of her companion, a woman insensitive enough to introduce an innocent to this sort of event. Couples were finding quiet corners and getting to know each other better, much better. Some of the ladies, and he used that term loosely, had already shed layers of clothing and their remaining garments were so thin that they revealed rather than concealed their shapes. Personally, he preferred to unwrap his presents, piece by piece, and he liked to do it in private rather than in an overcrowded room full of peers he didn't particularly like and took great pains to avoid.

Looking towards Lillian's position, Brent cursed his inattentiveness. The lady in red and her companion had disappeared. He pushed between companionable couples, past clutches of leering youths, and dodged ladies of the night who were advertising their wares so blatantly that the slightest movement would topple their breasts out of their bodices and into full view. Hell, if that green buck on his right peered any further down the neckline of that redhead's gown, they'd need to haul him out by his boots.

There, a laugh that sounded almost right for Lillian apart from a strange high-pitched trill at the end of every sentence, as if the speaker was deliberately leaving a question mark at the end of each speech. Nervousness? If it was Lillian, she had good reason to be nervous. And when Brent caught up with the two women, they'd have good reason to be nervous because he was furious with Lillian's unknown companion, and her.

Yes, he'd wanted his best friend to find happiness, but he'd envisaged her slowly renewing friendships next year in London, chaperoning her sister, and perhaps sometime in the future accepting a marriage proposal. The idea of any man making advances to her when her emotions were still raw after her husband's demise and the pain of the appalling rumors that said she'd urged her husband to his death, made his blood boil. Though he couldn't put his finger on why he was so incensed.

Lillian was his friend, nothing more, and she knew his

feelings about marrying again any time soon. She was also one of the few people who knew of his first wife's numerous affairs and what he'd done afterwards. He'd forgiven Marion for her affairs as his heart had never been truly engaged in their union and Marion had craved attention, constantly. What he couldn't forgive, never would, was emotionally wounded their daughter at every chance because she hated that Brent lavished his attention on their delightful daughter and not her. During the first months of their marriage, he'd tried. Very hard. But Celeste had become more and more obsessed her about her looks and had been horrified when her stomach had swelled with their child and silvery lines appeared across her trim abdomen. He'd assured her that he loved those streaks as they meant they'd soon be welcoming their child into the world, but she grew angrier with each month and by the time their daughter was ready to enter the world, Celeste had been throwing daily tantrums and heaping blame on Brent's head that carrying their child had ruined her figure. Being banned from her bedchamber had been grim, and yet a blessing, as by then he'd nearly used up his supply of patience and was simply biding his time until the baby arrived.

As he wove a path through the crowd, he listened for Lillian's voice and tried to smell her particular scent, though the air in the ballroom was thick with heavy scents from both females and males. The smell of desire, and arousal, swamped him as he squeezed around several couples in the final stages of negotiating the terms of their associations, with the women listing what they'd like their protectors to provide. A house, gowns, jewels, and visits to the theatre. The air reeked of sexual awareness, not something he'd been surrounded by for quite a long time and a smell he'd have gladly avoided for many more years.

The push and shove, and the manipulation and capitulation made him inwardly shudder. Though he'd visited his share of brothels and indulged himself at wild house parties in his younger years, he'd never employed a mistress. Swagger and boasting had been part of every young buck's introduction to society, both at London's upper class's balls and at country assemblies. Jostling and teasing during brothel visits had also been a normal part of his younger days. But then he'd married Marion and they'd added Margaret to their family and he'd been content to live the conservative life of a married man who believed in the sanctity of marriage. More recently, he'd simply felt jaded after one unhappy marriage and he couldn't dredge up excitement over two hundred primped and primed gentlemen and the equivalent number of ladies of the night playing games of intrigue and seduction.

There were many parts of married life he missed, desperately. Lust, desire, and passion he understood and, to be perfectly honest, yearned to experience again. The shared intimacy of conversations in bed after a bout of rigorous sex. Waking to a woman's soft body wrapped around him and taking his time rousing her from sleep and then making sweet slow love to her. That he missed. Fake relationships, the sort formed here, left him cold, yet he yearned for the connection and sense of belonging that came with having a lover, or being in love.

There! That voice. That was the voice he knew as well as his own, and the scent that had often tempted him to rethink his views on marriage. Maneuvering around the dozen men and six women surrounding her, Brent eased into the lady's intimate circle and stood at her shoulder. He sniffed. Oh, yes!

His senses hadn't led him astray, nor had his sanity deteriorated and tumbled into madness, where his imaginings spiraled out of control and his fantasies sprang to life. Lady Armstrong, Lillian, was truly here in the midst of this decadence and debauchery. He shifted so they stood shoulder to shoulder, their arms touching.

Leaning in, Brent whispered in Lillian's ear. 'Well, well, well. I certainly didn't expect to find you in attendance.'

*L*illian startled when a man spoke directly into her ear. She sucked in a deep breath. Heaven help her, but she recognized that deep and melodious voice.

Night after night she'd imagined that same voice soothing her when she cried over the death of man she'd imagined she'd loved, until his constant recklessness and his stream of women had cured her of the notion of loving him. Brent's imaginary voice had reiterated that she hadn't been responsible for her husband's death, and that she should hold her head high and ignore the gossips.

Lillian swiveled to see his face, her hand flying to her mouth in a dismal attempt to smother her gasp. She stared, stunned, at her neighbor and confidant, a known recluse who should be in Cornwall and putting his adorable daughter to bed.

Lillian's mind raced, scrabbling for an excuse for being here. Shock held her captive. Her best friend stood behind her and he'd recognized her, despite the pains she and Maggie had taken with their enormous masks and gowns purchased from the dressmaker who designed flamboyant gowns for courtesans. Lord Mallory, Brenton, was the last person she'd expect to meet at a ball for procuring a mistress.

Maggie, her companion and procurer of ball invitations, had assured her that the majority of gentlemen attending tonight would be vetted acquaintances of Lord Browning's. Gentlemen on the lookout for a new mistress, young men eager to exchange their quarterly allowances for a brief affair with a rising star in courtesan circles, or men with aspirations of wealth who hoped to afford a full time mistress in the next year or two.

Brenton didn't fit any of those categories or perhaps she was mistaken and he lived an entirely different life than the one she saw. He'd barely ventured ten miles from his estate in the past five or six years and preferred evenings at home with his daughter to roaming London's streets with his peers, gambling at clubs, or getting drunk and visiting brothels. She lifted her fan to her face and waved air across her heated cheeks, not wanting her male admirers to notice her distress. Maggie had promised that all conversations and connections were incognito, so Lillian wouldn't be recognized as the duke's disgraced daughter, giving her an opportunity to let the repressed side of Lillian to fly free.

The last thing she needed was a serious conversation with Brent, or to have him criticize or interfere in the outrageous night she and her companion had planned. Maggie had spoken about her previous experience attending a notorious ball a few months ago, after her own period of enforced mourning had finished. Maggie's twelve months of wearing depressing black and pretending to grieve for a man who'd been cruel and abusive had almost destroyed her, so she'd urged Lillian to avoid her mistakes.

Advised Lillian to avoid spending twelve or eighteen

months in seclusion and under censure from well-meaning but ignorant family members. Urged Lillian to do something rash and abnormal. Something to clear her mind and soul of the stink of her husband's infidelity, uncontrolled spending, and irrational actions.

Lillian, like Maggie, was already sick to the stomach with pretending her husband had been a saint when, in truth, he'd been controlling, unprincipled, and self-absorbed. And also like Maggie, Lillian blocked her ears when her late husband's family sang his praises, despite knowing his debts and obligations had depleted the family coffers and left them with a financial mess to clean up.

Why shouldn't she take the chance of a night's fun and freedom, hidden from high-society an out of reach of the duke's continual criticisms? She'd lost enough of her life married to a man who didn't deserve either her patience or her fortitude. Starting tonight, she'd take control of herself and rebirth the confident and happy person that only appeared now when she was staying at her father's country estate.

She'd been excited about this night for weeks and she'd no intention of running away before she'd explored and widened her experience, though only visually. Not even if Brenton threatened to expose her, or worse, visit her father and reveal where she'd been. Stiffening her spine, she took Brenton's hand and, after muttering a quick apology to her cluster of admirers, led him straight to one of the balcony doors. She didn't stop until they were in a darkened section of the balcony where no one could overhear their conversation.

She dropped his hand and turned to lean on the veranda rail and stared out at the garden. 'What are you doing here?'

She spoke without turning to face him, both mortified and terrified that he'd discovered her here.

'Michael dragged me here.' He caught her wrist and tugged her around to face him. 'Who is that woman you are with? Did she bring you here?' He ran his hand through his hair, trying to calm himself and dampen down his anger. 'Of course she brought you here. You wouldn't have known to come to a place like this otherwise. Did she coerce you in some way?'

Lillian chuckled. 'Do you truly believe me such an innocent that I don't know the location of brothels or the estate houses that hold balls where the main guests are ladies of the night? I'm not that naïve, Brent. When I was a married woman, the other married ladies spoke constantly about the state of their marriages. Those conversations included such things as where their husbands, fathers, or brothers went to visit paid women, and what happened in those places.' She snorted. 'They'd no idea that my own marriage was so dismal that the only times my husband touched me in bed was those rare occasions when he remembered he was supposed to breed a son and so made an appointment for the next night to visit my bedchamber. Even during those ten dreadful minutes he spent with me, he never thought to explain what happened between a man and a woman, or about how children were conceived. My mother, the duchess, gave me a one sentence explanation on my wedding day of how to act with my husband and the need to create a child, but she unfortunately never gave me the information I needed about what physical intimacy entailed, so the first time my husband lifted the hem of my night dress, I panicked.'

She heard Brent suck in a deep breath and knew he was horrified, and probably disgusted with her ignorance and stupidity. But as Brenton so often had, he surprised her.

'I'm so sorry. I should have realized that the duchess's instructions would be inadequate, and supplied you with more information. Lent you books. Prepared you for your first time being bedded by a man.'

'You?' She laughed. 'It was never your job to educate me, Brent. My husband was to blame for my inadequacies in bed, as he was for many other things. I accepted Geoffrey's proposal because I wanted my own household and to not remain under the duke's roof, though I only learned later about my husband's impetuous and self-centered character. As to what marriage, and intimacy, entailed, I was clueless.' She dipped her head. 'Apparently my parents knew that Gregory wasn't a very honorable man, yet they didn't see fit to inform me of his true nature. When I later complained of how he treated me, the duchess told me that a wife's duty was to accept whatever my husband did, and without complaint. Though to their credit, the worst of Geoffrey's character was known to only his closest cohorts and, as they were of the same ilk, they weren't about to reveal what they knew.'

'How did your husband treat you, in private?' Brent wouldn't meet her eyes when he asked the question.

She gasped. 'My God, not you too. You knew what Gregory was like and what he wanted in the bedroom.'

He reached for her hands, but she pulled away. Shocked and disappointed in her old confident, she couldn't stay. She spun towards the garden steps, picked up her skirts, and started to run.

'Lillian, no, please don't run from me.' He clasped her waist from behind as she reached the bottom of the steps and pulled her back against him, holding her still by crossing his arms over her chest. 'Stand still and listen to me. Please.' When she stopped wriggling and stood still in his arms, he said in a sad voice, 'I'd heard stories of Gregory's more extreme demands on the women he bedded, yes, but I'd no idea that he'd ask you to do those same things. If I'd known, I'd have--'

'What? Rushed to my rescue?' She snorted. 'I don't think so, not when British law declares me nothing more than my husband's chattel and allows him to do whatever he wishes with my mind and my body. Legally, no one could have saved me from Gregory's excesses. Not my parents, had they wanted to, and not my best friend. Though in all honesty, Geoffrey, for the most part, ignored and avoided me. He preferred lovers who also liked to push the boundaries. Dangerous dares between his friends, sharing lovers, and sex in public places. So I was glad when he died. Pleased that I'd never have to spend another day under the same roof as a man who treated women, and servants, as dirt beneath his feet. Relieved that he'd never again bang on my bedroom and demand admittance when he was so drunk he could barely stand. Or order me to leave my warm bed and go downstairs and entertain his also drunken friends at four in the morning. Or even, on one memorable occasion, order me to kneel before him on the cold floor, naked and shivering, because he'd bet that he could make a duke's daughter his slave.'

'I'm sorry, Lillian. So, so, sorry.'

'Oh, don't pity me over that. Thankfully, his companions had collapsed in drunken stupors in the entranceway and couldn't remember the bet in the morning. Neither could Geoffrey. Being naked and kneeling was rather exciting actually. It was the other part that I loathed.'

Brent's face paled. 'Wha...what other part?'

When he stumbled over the question, she was reminded that he'd been her friend for most of their lives, and even though he hadn't come to rescue, as she'd dreamed many times, he'd be furious on her behalf if she disclosed everything. Many times she'd wanted to share some of her hurt and shame with him, knowing that he'd understand and give comfort where he could, but she'd not wanted him to look upon her with revulsion. Not wanted him to know that she'd failed to give her husband what he preferred in the bedroom, and failed her parents by not giving them grandchildren.

She sucked in a breath. 'Even when he brought his hand down on my back and bottom, hard, I was intrigued rather than repulsed. I became excited at first, but then the pain always became too great and I screamed and cried, which angered Gregory. He told me, repeatedly, that other wives bore their punishment with good grace and made their husbands proud, whereas I yelled and sobbed and reminded him of a baby, and he didn't want to create a child with someone with such a pathetic nature. He wanted his children to be born from strength, not weakness.'

'I knew that Geoffrey's crowd sometimes chose women who liked a little rough treatment, but I never imagined he'd dishonor his marriage vows, and his wife, by causing her pain. Was nothing he did pleasurable for you?'

She shrugged. 'As I said, he cared little for me and what I needed. Two weeks before he died, he dragged me out of bed and pushed me to the floor on my stomach, with all his weight pressed on my back as he pushed himself inside me. I cried because it hurt and when he noticed the blood, he insisted it was normal part of marriage and that I was abnormal because I bled.'

'Christ Almighty, he took you like an animal.' He

gripped his head in his hands, his face contorted in agony. 'I'd no idea it was so bad. Did you tell him that he hurt you?'

She nodded. 'Yes.'

'Yet he showed no remorse?'

She nodded again. 'At times he became obsessed with planting his seed in me so that I would conceive, though only at his family's urging. So after I had my courses, he'd visit me.'

'What about the bleeding? Did he summon a doctor?'

'No. He didn't want anyone to know.'

'I'm not surprised, considering he brutalized you.'

'I was Geoffrey's wife, so as he said, he could do whatever pleased him.'

'Huh, so he practically raped his wife, used you as brood mare each month, and enjoyed doing so. A man whose preferences were depraved and should never have been brought home to the marriage bed. Even some brothels forbid entry to men who harm their girls.'

'Brent, I was his wife.' She shrugged. 'His chattel.'

He shucked in an audible breath. 'Taking a woman from behind can be pleasurable for both parties. But forcing a woman, wife or not, to accept him forcibly, against her will, is rape. Wife or not. He didn't deserve a wife like you.'

Lillian smiled at Brent's vehemence on her behalf. 'It's over now, my friend, so don't feel enraged on my behalf. Be pleased for me because I'm now free to enjoy some of the pleasurable things that men do with women. I've listened to women who crave amorous attention from their husbands, or lovers, so I understand that what happened in my marital bed wasn't normal.' She ran her gloved hand down his cheek, hoping to elicit a smile. 'I have tonight, and many more nights, to make up for what I missed.'

'But this isn't the right place for you to test the waters.'

He waved a hand towards the ball room and the noise from a hundred animated conversations. 'One day soon, you'll meet a man who loves you, and who wants to marry you and adore you. Let him teach you about pleasure. Anything you see, or hear, tonight will also be leaning towards perversion. Some things here will shock you, even if you think of yourself as experienced.' He took her hand and lightly shook it. 'Let me call Michael's carriage to take you home. Or find your companion and insist that she leaves with you.'

She laughed softly. 'You'll never convince her to leave early. She's attended a party like this once before, and was enthralled. Neither of us knew that women could enjoy being with a man, but she discovered that here and she wants to flirt and have fun, and if it leads to something more, then so be it. We're ready.'

'What can I say to convince you to leave, now, before masks are removed and identities revealed. You'll be shocked to find how many gentlemen of your acquaintance are here tonight.'

'I've already recognized many men, and ladies, by their hair and voices.'

'See! If you've uncovered people's identities, they'll be able to do the same. They'll recognize your voice, and your coloring.' He touched her hair. 'If you leave now, they won't be certain it was you. If you stay, everyone will know and the gentlemen will treat you differently tomorrow.'

She narrowed her gaze. 'How do you know so much about courtesan's balls? I suppose you've attended many since your wife passed away.'

He groaned. 'You know that's not true. I prefer to stay away from this sort of...' He waved his hand towards the ballroom.

'Romp? Orgy?'

He covered her mouth with his large hand and she closed her eyes and sighed. Even the leather of his evening gloves and the sleeve of his coat smelled of horses and paddocks and Brent. An outdoor man who loved the country and riding and whose clothes carried his manly aroma, evening at a soiree. She'd always felt safe when he was with her, and tonight was no exception. Her head had been held high when she'd entered the candlelit ball room, but her bravery was a pretense and inside she quaked and her stomach clenched. Brent's voice had immediately soothed her stretched nerves. If he was with her, nothing bad would happen, of that she was confident.

'Brent,' she murmured as she entwined her fingers with his and gave him a begging look. 'If I promise we'll leave in an hour or two and not stay until dawn, will you keep my secret. Let me have a couple of hours here to watch and learn and...'

He frowned. 'And what? Has your companion, whose name I still don't know, made some sort of arrangement?' He looked worried and suspicious, and with good right. Perhaps she'd reveal half of their plans, enough to pacify him and give them room to explore without him hovering like a distraught father.

'Please, let me go on my way. You can do whatever you came for, too.'

His hands were on his hips and he looked angry. 'I did not come here to find a mistress, if that's what you're thinking. I'm more than happy to leave now and take you home.'

She mimicked his stance by putting her hands on her own hips and scowling at him. 'I am not leaving. Not until I've explored all the upper rooms as well.'

'The upper rooms? Are you mad? A lady cannot go

prowling around the bedrooms. There will be couples in those bedrooms having--'

'Having sex? I do know these things. I'm a widow, not a spinster.'

'Huh! And what will you do if you walk into a room where there are more than two people? Perhaps three or four, or even five, in one bed.'

'Oooh, do you know which rooms they are in?'

'I do not. And I don't wish to know.' He sucked in a breath and pointed a finger at her face. 'And neither do you.'

'I'm my own person now and I'll do what I want. I'm going upstairs to explore, and to observe. To join in if I'm asked.'

'You deserve better than the men you'll find here, Lillian. Go to a respectable ball. Dance with some decent men. Find another husband.'

'Why are you eager for me to risk a repeat of my miserable marriage, when you've declared that you'll never marry again?'

'Because you're a woman and I'm a man.'

Her eyes narrowed. 'That's a very biased view, and I thought you better than that.'

He groaned. 'You're right. It's unfair to tell you to risk more unhappiness when I won't.'

'Everyone knows you're avoiding your family because they push eligible ladies towards you. They want you to remarry and give your daughter a new mother.'

'They've no right to interfere in our lives, mine or my daughter's. We're happy as we are, the two of us.'

'Your wife hurt you, deeply, and so you've refused to even speak to the women your mother thinks suitable.'

'I speak to you.'

'Only because I visit you and drag you away from your

house to go riding. I refuse to let you retreat from the world. You're a wonderful man with a lot to give to another woman. To another wife.'

'You're the only lady that I can tolerate being near for more than ten minutes.'

'And you're the only man I'd select for a second husband, and you're against marriage.' She looked towards a group of men smoking at the far end of the verandah. 'Hence my venture into the unknown tonight. The sedate balls are full of married men or old lechers, as all the exciting men are here instead.' She pointed towards the cluster of five or six young men. 'Perhaps one of them might be the boost I need to restore my faith in the male gender. A virile young man who knows about pleasurable sex.'

He scowled as he watched the young men laugh and slap each other on the back. 'Those pups are too inexperienced to give a woman pleasure. At that age, it's all over too quickly. You need someone who knows how to revere every dip and curve of your body. Arouse you and keep you on edge for hours, and then leave you limp with pleasure as the sun rises.' He shook his head and seemed to collect himself.

She swallowed. Yes, she'd often imagined Brent doing those very things to her body and she didn't doubt that he knew many ways to make sex exciting and unforgettable, but there was no point imagining herself with Brent when she knew how studiously he avoided contact with women these days. Well, except for her and his cook.

'Not all men are cruel,' he was saying when she paid attention to his words rather than the way his trousers stretched across his groin when he had his hands on his hips and his coat tails pulled aside. 'Some husbands value their wives and treat them like queens.'

She sighed. 'A nice thought, Brent, but unless you can introduce me to one of those paragons of husbands, I'm reduced to finding my excitement with one of the gentlemen here tonight.'

'Lillian,' he hissed through gritted teeth. 'Have you been paying attention to me? I know most of the gentlemen attending this ball and there isn't one of them that's good enough for you.'

'Not even you?' At his shocked look, she waved her hand between them. 'Sorry. I know you're not interested in me. Not in that way, anyway.'

She watched his Adam's apple bob as he swallowed, hard. Was she mistaken? Did he find her attractive, after all? Because, Lord knew, she found him, and his muscled body, very enticing. Many a time she'd ridden behind him purposely so she could watch his taut behind rise and fall in the saddle, his thighs stretched tight as he rose slightly in the stirrups and his coat pulling across wide shoulders. She'd secretly been pleased that he wouldn't allow visitors to his house, declaring that he and his daughter were still grieving. Though she knew that was a fabrication to prevent his mother from bringing a constant stream of eligible ladies to visit, she enjoyed being the only woman who saw him dressed down and carefree as they rode together. Which they did often.

With her head tilted to one side so she could peer up at him, she said, 'Are you? Interested in me that way? As a woman.'

She heard the hiss of his indrawn breath and sensed she was about to be rejected. Being rejected by her husband had wounded her feminine pride, though even that pain hadn't destroyed her. By contrast, if her best friend, the man that knew her better than her mother, turned away from her, the pain would kill her. She spun towards the door, desperate to escape.

'Ah, there you are.' Her companion, Maggie, stepped through the balcony doorway and strode towards her. She eyed Brenton, slowly appraising him from top to toe, before turning her back to him. 'I was worried when I couldn't find you. Are you all right?'

Brenton stepped around Maggie and gave her the same disdainful look as she'd given him. He gave a small bow and said, 'I'm Brenton. And your name is...?'

Maggie rolled her eyes. 'I know better than to reveal myself here. And I already know who you are, my lord.'

Lillian squirmed when Brent's gaze flicked towards her and back to Maggie. 'I've told my friend about you, Brent.'

'I see.' He turned to Maggie and leaned in close. 'And what sort of friend are you that you brought a young woman to an event that caters to less than respectable ladies?'

'The best sort, my lord.' Maggie didn't flinch form Brent's blunt question. 'The sort of friend who recognizes that a woman has been scarred by men and life and needs a chance to enjoy herself without censure. Needs a night of fun and frolic, rather than one of fear and loneliness.'

'Loneliness?' Brent repeated the word in surprise and looked at Lillian. 'Is she correct? You've been lonely.'

'In my marriage, yes, I was lonely. Geoffrey didn't like me to see my own friends or family too much. He wanted me at home, where he could keep me under control, or attending events on his arm. A decorative addition to enhance his reputation as a man who purchased only the best quality goods. Immaculate clothing, flashy carriage, well-bred horses, and a household where he ruled supreme. There was little room for me to breathe.'

He touched her arm. 'I'm sorry to have failed you so

badly. I was so swept up in my own misery and battling to keep my wife's affairs under wraps that I gave no thought to how your life was when in London. I picture you as that free spirit riding across the fields at full pelt and not giving a damn who sees you in your breeches and shirt.'

'Come inside,' Maggie urged. 'We shall investigate the secrets of the upper floors.'

'No, you won't,' Brent said sharply. 'Perhaps you are accustomed to this level of debauchery, madam, but Lillian will not witness what goes on up there. The punch is heavily laced and everyone will be tossing off their inhibitions, if they had any to start with.

'You didn't tell me his lordship was a prude, Lillian,' Maggie said, making Lillian groan aloud. Her friend was taunting Brent, though she had no idea why, nor what she should do to intervene.

Brent stiffened. 'I am far from a prude. I simply don't think any of these men, or the sights, are worthy of Lillian. She deserves a gentleman, not a lout. A man who will introduce her to pleasure and block out her memories of pain.'

'Then perhaps, your lordship, you should volunteer to broaden her knowledge of bedroom antics.'

Brent's eyes widened and Lillian held her breath waiting for him to laugh at her companion's suggestion, or perhaps berate her. He met her gaze and the heat in his sent blood rushing through her entire body and a flush rush to her cheeks.

'Perhaps I should. At least Lillian would be safe with me.'

Lillian gasped. 'Would you two mind not discussing me when I'm standing beside you.'

To her shock, they continued their conversation as if she was invisible.

'That's true, your lordship, but you're her best friend. You risk her falling in love with you.'

Brent shrugged. 'It's a risk I'm willing to take if it means smuggling her out of here before anyone recognizes her.' He stared at Maggie. 'Will you leave with us?'

Lillian had heard enough. She walked away and left them discussing her. Once back inside the ballroom, she pasted on her most flirtatious smile and eased her way into the closest circle of masked revelers. The gentlemen automatically shifted to widen the circle and allow her into their conversational ring, eager to speak with an unknown woman.

'Would one of you lovely gentlemen mind escorting me to the upper levels. I'd go alone but I'd rather an escort who understands these things.' She fluttered her eyelashes and tiptoed her fingers up the sleeve of the blonde man on her right. 'Which of you will introduce me to the games I've been told take place in the upper chambers.' She turned to the dark haired man on her left and ran her hand along his sleeves, trying to flutter her eyelashes again in what she hoped was a seductive manner. Though by the alarmed looks on the men's faces, she feared she was a failure as a temptress. Time for more explicit advances, and damn the consequences. Time to toss off her conventional persona and welcome some excitement into her life.

Her hand eased further up the dark man's sleeve and curled it around his neck, tugging his face down to hers. She kissed his freshly-shaved cheek and was gratified to hear his breath catch and feel his hands slide around her waist to draw her close to his body.

'Stop.' When someone yelled near her ear, the delicious dark-haired man abruptly dropped his hands from her body. He looked over his shoulder and Lillian followed his gaze. Brent gripped his elbow from behind, tight enough to cause the poor young man to pale and tremble.

She whacked at Brent's hand where he gripped the man's sleeve. 'Let go of him,' she hissed. 'This instant.'

Brent released the young man and he and his group of friends backed away and then moved along to the next empty area and continued their conversation, glancing at Brent and obviously talking about their connection, and most worrying, their identities. Gentleman were much easy to distinguish here because their own concession to anonymity was a short black mask, whereas the women could dress in a completely style than their usual and thus radically change their appearance. Her low-cut red gown was something a bird of paradise looking for her next prey would wear, and not the style of gown Lillian wore to tonnish events.

'How dare you.' She spat the words at Brent and gave him her fiercest glare. 'You shouldn't have interfered like that. If those gentlemen recognize you, they might work out who I am, which is exactly what you wanted to avoid.' She huffed. 'Besides, I instigated that kiss.'

'Why would you do such a brazen thing? Risk your good name and your life in such an impulsive manner.'

She sighed, all her anger delating. 'My good name evaporated when Geoffrey's sexual preferences became known after his death. The men he mixed with kept his secrets when he was alive, and possibly even liked whips and ropes as much as Geoffrey, but dead men can't reveal their secrets so they felt safe to expose him, while distancing themselves from those activities.'

'But why would they risk incriminating themselves?'

'I learned later that two girls had died, a day apart and in different areas of London, but both had been physically tormented and their bodies were left in parks in Mayfair. Government officials were sent to investigate after a minister's wife and children stumbled upon one of them, and there was a push to find the culprit and to close down any houses of ill repute in respectable neighborhoods.'

'I read about the murders, but surely they don't think Geoffrey had anything to do with that. He wasn't the most respected man and nor was he a decent husband, but I cannot imagine him killing women.'

'The enquiry cleared Geoffrey, but as those houses were places that Geoffrey and his cohorts visited, his so-called friends decided to toss out Geoffrey's name and draw the scrutiny away from them.'

Brent took her hands and shook them lightly. 'Why didn't you tell me?'

She shrugged. 'Geoffrey was dead and I simply wanted to forget all the sordidness and start afresh.' She waved a hand at the guests, whose conversations had become bawdier and louder the more punch was consumed and, as inhibitions were drowned in liquor, both women and men had stripped away clothing and were well on their way to public sex. 'Here, I can reclaim myself, because everyone indulges in excesses and they don't judge each other badly because they've let down their guards for an evening. Look around you.' She pointed to a curtained alcove across for them. 'Lord Hastings has been in there for twenty minutes with a lady. Actually, a young girl.'

'Hastings is the son of a duke so he has plenty of blunt to purchase a mistress, or two. And though he's known to prefer young blondes, he rewards the girls well and he'd never harm them.' He looked her in the eyes and spoke with sincerity. 'Every woman, or girl, invited tonight comes willingly, and knows what to expect. News of these balls is kept secret from the sticklers, but many women are off the streets because they're kept by men.'

She glanced from his polished evening shoes to his perfectly-tied cravat. His vest was shot with gold, his coat of the finest deep blue wool, and his accessories of a stick pin and fob watch looked expensive. 'You must be in demand. You're handsome, wealthy, and well-presented.'

He chuckled. 'My valet took extra care with my accouterments. As to the rest, I'm flattered that you think me handsome.'

She rolled her eyes. 'You've noticed the women looking you over as much as I have.'

'I've no desire for a mistress.'

She frowned. 'What do you want? You can't shut yourself away for ever, you know.'

Creases appeared between his brows while he considered his answer, and those lines added to his appearance as a gentleman of distinction and experience. Whenever she was this close, she longed to lay her hands on his chest and feel the vitality that pumped through his strong body. She knew his legs and arms were strong and muscled for riding, but she wanted to feel his heart pumping and to absorb his heat and energy. Would he be shocked if she accepted the invitation he'd blithely tossed out earlier?

She'd ignored it at the time because she'd be mortified if she said yes and discovered that he hadn't been serious. After two hours in this enervated gathering, watching and learning, her own excitement had risen to such a state that her body clamored for more and her mind whirled with the possibilities of what she might try, and with whom. In reality, the person she'd most like to engage in a bout of earthy sex with stood beside her, unaware that her fantasies always included Brent as her hero, her masterful seducer, and her introduction to the gratification she'd been denied during her marriage.

'I want,' he said, breaking her reverie and forcing her attention back to her question. 'I want what any man wants. A home, a wife, and children. But if I take a second wife, she'll be sweet and biddable and faithful. The complete opposite of Marion.' He grinned. 'Somewhat like you, though you're never biddable.'

She pretended to be outraged, despite knowing it was the truth. Her parents said she was too stubborn for her own good, her sisters said she argued too much, and Geoffrey... He'd put her to her knees and whipped her bottom to bend her will and force her to submit to him, body and mind. Bowing to a dominant husband had been rather exciting, so if Geoffrey had stopped at light trails of the whip ends across her bare body she'd have been tantalized and aroused, but his tastes had been extreme and their night-time interludes had ended with tears and pain and the embarrassment of inventing explanations for the blood on her clothes when they stuck to the raw slashes across her back the next day.

Money had sealed the lips of her maid, but she couldn't bribe all the servants without exposing herself and the truth about her marriage. Servants gossiped, and she feared that her parents would learn how she'd been subdued by her husband, though intervening would have been illegal because the law stated that a husband could beat his wife, within limits. Geoffrey had stretched those limits and investigators had visited her house and asked her questions, but by then it was too late. Her sadistic husband was dead. She only hoped that the murderer of the two prostitutes would be caught before he killed again.

She smiled. 'No, I'm not normally biddable, but if you

take me upstairs I'll submit to you. Do whatever you like with me while in this house, and tomorrow we'll pretend it never happened.'

'Doing whatever I want with you, Lillian, would change our relationship forever. We could never go back to being good neighbors who shared their news. If I have you once, I'll want more. I know that. Have known it for a long time, which is why I've trained myself to keep a respectable distance between us. As it is, I knew you were in attendance this evening because I recognized your perfume. I was aroused before I ever found you, the way I always am when you're around.'

She gasped. 'Why have you not said something?'

'Because being able to discuss things with you, estate matters, politics, our peers, has kept me sane. My family believes that my daughter occupies all my thoughts, and time, but they're wrong. You've occupied my thoughts far more than they know.'

Her chest felt tight and her breathing strained. 'What sort of thoughts have you had about me?'

'Sexual ones. Very erotic. Are you shocked?' She shook her head, unable to reply. 'I'd like to take you upstairs to a bedchamber and show you how much I need you, and for more than friendship. But...'

'But what? We both want the same thing, so what's holding you back?'

'Being intimate often begets certain expectations for women.'

She frowned. 'I don't understand.'

He let out a ragged breath. 'I'm not making myself clear, I know. I've vowed to never marry for love again, to never risk the devastation that often comes with that emotion, especially if one partner loves and the other doesn't.'

'You're remembering your wife, but I'm nothing like her. I may be a little strong willed--'

'A little?' He laughed.

'Very well. Somewhat strong willed, but I was never unfaithful to my husband, and I would never shame my marriage vows by having an affair.'

He tangled his fingers in her hair and brought her face close to his. 'I know, and that's the problem. If we're intimate, you'll expect more from me than I might be able to give in return. You're the warmest and most giving person I know, and you deserve to loved in return. You deserve more than my respect and admiration.'

She shook her head. 'You already treat me far better than Geoffrey ever did, and that means a lot to me. So we'll speak no more of poetic love and we'll give our bodies to each other as freely as the courtesans do with their protectors.'

'Doing that demeans your life, your station as a lady.'

She smiled. 'Not if it's what I want, what I need.' She ran her hands up and down his arms, squeezing his muscled forearms and making him groan. 'I'm desperate to see you unclothed. To touch and explore you.'

Brent groaned again. Lillian and the warmth she radiated always charmed him, but in this setting where they were free to explore their desires, his resistance crumbled. Despite knowing that keeping Lillian at arm's length would be impossible if they shared this one fantasy-fulfilling night, he'd used up all his half-hearted arguments regarding them walking up that staircase together. If her family discovered that he'd taken her to bed instead of tossing her over his shoulder and taking her home, they'd shoot him anyway. Yet, he found her impossible to resist.

She took his hand and started towards the steps and he

followed like an obedient dog. Two hours ago he'd been protesting about attending this ball, yet now he wanted to scoop Lillian into his arms and run up the stairs so she couldn't change her mind. For the next few hours, she was his and he intended enjoying every moment she was in his arms.

Guilt would come tomorrow, though not regret. No matter what happened here, he could never regret hearing that she thought him handsome, when he'd thought she'd never viewed him as more than a friendly neighbor. And when she'd said she wanted to see him unclothed, his trousers had tightened over his swelling groin and he could only think of releasing her breasts and worshipping them as he'd longed to do. Of revealing her curves to his gaze and being able to touch her soft skin.

He smirked as he squeezed her hand. 'So, you think I'm handsome?'

She laughed and gave his hand a tug to hurry him along. 'Discussions like that would be better held in private, don't you think?'

A laughing couple rushed past them, stopping every few steps to kiss and giggle, before they urged each other up the next level. Lillian hoped there was an abundance of rooms on the higher levels of the house, because she'd seen many couples, and threesomes, race up the stairs as if they'd suddenly decided to savor every minute of the hours left until dawn. And idea that held a lot of appeal, considering the man she'd admired..., no, the man she'd wanted in her bed for a long time was currently gripping her hands and urging her up the steps too.

3

Brent pulled Lillian to a halt when they reached the first floor balcony and swung her around and into his arms. He held the back of her head while he dipped his mouth and kissed her, soundly. 'Better to get our first kiss out the way so there's no embarrassment when we find an empty room.'

When he slowly pulled away, she sucked in a deep breath and stared up at him with wide eyes. Her fingers touched her lips, moving across them with reverence, and she swallowed, hard. Seeing the affect their first kiss had on Lillian was an aphrodisiac, making Brent's cock stir and throb and beg for relief.

He pressed one thigh between Lillian's legs and tilted his pelvis, pushing his erection into her warmth and telling her feel how much she aroused him. Letting her know how much he wanted her, and her sexy body. Their next kiss was hungrier, more demanding, and as he drew back, he breathed in her familiar citrus scent and rejoiced at her ragged breathing and the quick rise and fall of her chest pressed against his.

Good, she sounded as abstracted as he felt, and after only two kisses. A night of these stirring kisses and touches might kill them both but, damn it all, they both deserved one night of happiness, one night of sin. His mind raced with a dozen ways he'd please her, in addition to the dozen ways he wanted to claim her body.

Face to face so he could see her when she climaxed, from behind so he could lick her spine and play with her nipples, and yes, since the moment she'd mentioned kneeling before Geoffrey he'd envisioned Lillian on her knees. Though unlike her brutal husband, he'd ensure that she enjoyed offering herself because he'd gladly do the same. Kneel before her and worship her body, bringing her to peak after peak and demonstrating that a man and woman could explore sexually, push the boundaries, but as equals. Displaying trust in each other and having faith that neither would be hurt.

Taking Lillian's arm, he hurried her down the corridor and past closed doors on each side. 'We need to find an empty room before anyone else comes along here. It's narrow enough that we cannot avoid coming into close contact with people and therefore there's a bigger risk of someone seeing us together and connecting us.'

At each door he stopped, and listened. Squeals and giggles and moans made it easy to distinguish which rooms were occupied and what they were doing and he didn't want to linger and cause embarrassment for Lillian, though from what she'd revealed about her late husband, Lillian's innocence had been stripped from her during her sham of a marriage. Geoffrey had been a bastard who deserved to rot in hell for the damage he'd done to his sweet wife, and Brent longed to erase her bad memories and replace them with more amicable ones.

No noise came from beyond the last door on the left so Brent knocked softly and paused, enjoying the feel of Lillian's hand gripping his and the warmth of her body pressed against him as they waited. No one answered his knock and there were no voices, or squeals, so he opened the door and gestured for Lillian to enter. She walked past him and towards the bed, stopping to run her hand over the plush covering and swiveling around to obverse the rest of the room's furnishings. He leant against the closed door and smiled.

'It's a beautiful room.'

'I'm not looking at the room, or Browning's furnishings, but what I see is certainly beautiful. Stunning, in fact.'

Lillian laughed, but then covered her mouth with her hands. 'You don't need to compliment me or seduce me with words, Brent, because I came with you willingly. In fact, I should be seducing you out of your worries.'

He stood in front of her and spread his arms wide, grinning, and feeling lighter of heart than he had in a long while. 'Please, feel free to do what you want with me.' He shrugged out of his coat and tossed it over his shoulder towards the door, careless of where it landed. His entire focus was one the extraordinary lady who stood before him, biting her lower lip, and frowning. He held out his hand and when she took it, he tugged her closer. 'What's the matter?'

'I...I've realized that I don't know how to seduce a man, any man, and especially not you.'

He brushed his lips lightly across Lillian's. 'Why especially me?'

'Because...because I want to make you happy. To make this perfect.' She pulled off her gloves and put them onto the bedside table. 'This might be the only night we have together, so I want it to be ...memorable.'

He copied her movements and put his gloves on the table beside hers, smiling at the picture of their belongings touching each other and was seized by a yearning to view that small intimacy more often, perhaps on a permanent basis. Sliding his bare hands around her waist was also an unexpected delight, as it'd been more than four years since he'd touched a woman who wasn't a family member. 'Anything and everything we do will be memorable, and as for seducing me, you accomplished that the moment you asked me to come upstairs. I'm entranced by your loveliness and in thrall to your proposal.'

Kissing her stopped her from answering for a moment, and when he lifted his head her gorgeous gray eyes were glazed and her cheeks flushed a becoming pink. Slipping his hands around her head, he pulled out her pins, one by one, and dropped them to the carpet. A mass of curls tumbled to her shoulders and he groaned. 'I haven't seen your hair down since we were children.' He lifted a long lock to his face and inhaled. 'I recognized your citrus scent. Though at first I imagined one of your sisters, Candace most likely, had inveigled an invitation to the ball, or had been escorted here by an ungentlemanly rake.'

'Oh. You didn't know it was me?'

'Not at first, no, but when I came closer and saw--'

'What?'

He rolled his eyes. 'This is a little embarrassing, but your breasts are quite... unique.' As he spoke, he rolled his thumbs across her bodice and stroked her nipples through the fabric. 'Unique and quite exquisite.' He turned her and started on the back buttons, stopping as he released each one to ease her gown aside and nibble a path across her shoulders. Lillian moaned and his prick jumped and swelled.

She pushed her bottom back until she found his arousal and then she wriggled. His turn to moan, aloud, and grip her waist to hold her still. 'Sweetheart, as amazing as that feels, I need you naked before I lose control, toss you on your back and take you, hard and fast.'

'I wouldn't mind.' She pulled her bodice down her shoulders and bared her pale skin.

His mouth went dry. 'But I would mind. Later, I'll have you bent over the dressing table and plough you from behind.' She hissed in a breath. 'And hard and fast up against the wall. Then with your bare back to the window and the curtains open so that anyone standing in the court-yard can watch and wish they were the lucky bastard having unrestrained sex with the most skilled courtesan at the ball. They won't know that by day you're the daughter of a duke observing the conventions of mourning, because they'll hear you scream out your climax and spread tales of witnessing the spiciest bird of paradise in the whole of Britain in action.'

Lillian's breathing was a series of pants and she slumped against his chest. 'Brent, please, I need you. Hurry ... hurry.'

'Shush, my love. We have all night.' He worked on the ties and clasps of her remaining clothing, letting everything puddle at her feet before helping her step away from her coverings and into his arms. Her thin chemise hid nothing from his hungry eyes and when she crossed her arms over her chest, he gently pulled them aside. 'Let me look, my sweet. After all these years of wondering, and longing, I finally get to feast on these.' He hefted her breasts in his palms and moaned. 'Superb. Truly magnificent.'

He slipped his hands under the hem and slid the lawn upwards, inch by inch, while she quivered under his hands. The chemise joined her other discarded clothing and he stepped back, still holding her hands, and surveyed the splendor he'd unveiled. She shivered and burrowed into his chest. 'Are you cold?'

She shook her head.

'Excited?'

She nodded.

'Good. So am I, and a little nervous.'

She chuckled. 'I'm sure you're very knowledgeable and not at all nervous.'

'I haven't been with a woman since my wife died.'

'Four years?'

He nodded. 'And even more than that. After she'd admitted to being unfaithful, several times, I could no longer stand being in the same room as her, let alone the same bed.' Unable to resist her upturned face and her red lips, he wrapped his hands through her hair and poured all his newly-revealed feeling into his kisses. 'Tell me how to make this good for you.'

She licked her lips. 'Take off your clothes, Brent. Please.'

He grinned as he peeled off his cravat, vest, and shirt as quickly as he could, sitting on the side of the bed to tug off his boots and stockings and rising again to step out of his smalls. Her eyes were as wide as saucers and her mouth hung open, making him feel like a god. 'See anything you like?'

She nodded. 'I like everything I see. Can I...can I touch you?'

Lillian reached towards his erection and ran a tentative finger down the length. He closed his eyes and savored the light touch, knowing nothing had ever felt as good as having the person he was closest to, apart from his daughter, put her soft hands on his body. His penis bobbed and she laughed. He covered her hand with his and wrapped them around his shaft, hissing in a breath and squeezing. Showing her what he liked. 'That's so good,' he murmured, 'And yet not enough. Not nearly enough.'

He nudged her back wards towards the top of the bed. 'Lie down.' Holding her wrists, he eased her back onto the thick quilt, leaving her legs dangling over the side, but when he pressed her thighs apart with his palms she jumped and her head rose from the bed.

She stared at him. 'What are you doing?'

Brent frowned. 'I assumed your husband would have done these things with you.' He waved towards her exposed sex and her swollen labia. Unable to help himself, he ran a finger through her crease and sighed when he found her soaking wet. 'If he didn't bring you to orgasm this way, Lillian, then he robbed you of one of the most pleasurable things a woman can experience. Let me show you.' Her muscles relaxed and he gently used his thumbs to spread her wide enough to give him a better view. Blood raced to his groin and he swelled, harder than when he'd sighted her rounded breasts. His chest tightened as he looked his fill at her centre and admired her pink and swollen folds. 'You want me.'

Her eyes were squinted and her answer was a whisper. 'Yes. Please. Now.'

'Look at me Lillian and tell me that you won't regret this tomorrow, because in another few minutes I doubt I'll be able to stop. Not when you're spread open and ready to welcome me into your body. Not when you're all I can see and think about.'

She swallowed and nodded. 'I do...'

She cleared her throat and his own tightened with emotion. Never had he imagined that he'd have the chance to make love to his best friend, and never had he wanted a woman more. When he'd married he'd been infatuated with his wife, though it had taken only a few months to discern that the sweet and congenial Marion he knew was a façade and nothing like the nasty and conniving female she revealed herself to be after she wore his ring and carried his name.

Her voice was stronger the second time. 'I do want you and there will be no regrets tomorrow. Not from me, at least.' She looked at him with a question in her eyes.

He shook his head. 'I'm honored that you want to be with me and no, I'll never regret any time we have together. This night is already the best I've spent in many moons.' He bent and ran his tongue up her outer wetness before dipping the tip into her crevice. "You taste good and you feel amazing.' He slid two fingers inside and wiggled them. She gave a soft squeal of astonishment and, hopefully, enjoyment, so he did it again and again until she writhed on the bed, hips lifting, and breathing shortened. 'So beautiful and so close,' he murmured, 'feeling like a king for rousing so much passion in someone trained from birth to show no public displays of emotion.

His lover's mouth opened and he knew she was about to shatter with her release, his level of excitement rising with hers. Nothing would please him more than to hear her scream his name as she orgasmed, long and hard.

'Bloody hell.' He withdrew his fingers, pushed her legs together, and straightened, all in one movement. Grasping her wrists, he tugged her upright. 'Someone's coming,' he hissed beside her ear, 'And our masks are gone.'

Her hand half-smothered her gasp but her eyes were wide with fright, and her cheeks had lost all their previously-pink color. Thinking fast, Brent kicked what clothing he could reach with his foot under the bed, scooped Lillian up and tossed her over his shoulder. The room had no where to hide but a large wardrobe at one end of the rectangular room and he prayed that it wasn't filled with clothing. On the way, he grabbed other garments from the floor and strode to the cupboard, wrenching open the doors.

'Thank God,' he muttered, as he tipped Lillian over to stand on her feet inside the half empty hanging space. Clothing was tossed to one side and he stepped in with Lillian, having to press tightly against her to close the door behind him. Shivers wracked her body and he glanced at the floor, using his toe to shift the garments in the hope of finding something to cover her nakedness. The chattering of her teeth sounded loud in the silence and he put his finger to her lips to urge her to muffle the sound. She nodded and put her finger between her teeth. 'Jesus, don't bite yourself.' Worry for her had his mind spinning but he spotted a scarf draped over a hanging nail and used it to wrap her neck and slide it between her teeth.

She gave him a grateful smile but dropped the scarf from her mouth when the door was flung open so hard that it hit the wall. Tucking the scarf between her teeth, he lifted his white shirt from the floor and eased it over her head, sliding each arm into the sleeves slowly and carefully. Lillian sensed his caution and followed his lead until the short hem dropped to her thighs. Relief overwhelmed him and he thanked the deities that at least she'd be covered if one of the intruders opened the wardrobe doors.

Taking one end of the silk scarf, he indicated how it could be pulled across her face as a replacement to the mask and she gave a nod of acknowledgement. Her easy acceptance of the situation and his instructions boosted his opinion of her intelligence, though he'd always known she was exceptional for a lady of the peerage. The duke, her father, had a low opinions of females who showed initiative and intellect and his censure had pushed Lillian to spend most of her time at the duke's country estate, for which Brent had always been thankful.

Her face creased with worry lines and, thinking she was still cold, he rubbed her arms from wrists to shoulder with his bare hands. A head shake told him he was incorrect, and a finger pointed at his bared chest, and his exposed groin, led him to the answer. Sweet Lillian, his Lillian, was worrying about him, rather than her own predicament. His face split into a huge grin, which also puzzled her as she frowned harder.

'Later,' he whispered in her ear.

When they were out of danger from discovery, he'd explain how much he admired her and her compassion for others. Few tonnish ladies would have coped in a wardrobe and would most likely be screaming loudly enough to bring every guest running. His late wife would have berated him, loudly, if they'd been caught in this situation, although with him she'd acted conservatively and almost prudishly for most of their marriage, another reason her affairs had been such a shock to him. Marion acting impulsively, slinking off to clandestine assignations that made no sense to him, leading him to the miserable conclusion that something lacking in his character had pushed her into affairs with married men. His cross to bear, and his alone.

Loud voices sounded in the bedchamber and he and Lillian put their ears to the wooden panel to listen. A woman, or perhaps two, were giggling and shrieking while at least two male voices issued orders, though with a hint of amusement lightening their gruff commands. The handle lifted from the catch silently and Brent opened the wardrobe door a fraction, allowing them to catch more of the silly conversation and to sneak a glimpse of their unwanted intruders.

Damn his stupidity for not checking that the door from the corridor was properly locked, and for being so caught up in thoughts of Lillian's luscious curves that he must have neglected to turn the key fully in the lock.

'Lucky I have a key to all the rooms,' a male voice announced, and he could see a key dangling from the fingertips of a gentleman.

He grimaced, and at Lillian's look of concern whispered, 'Browning. Master key.' Thankfully the scarf covered her shocked gasp. How unlucky could they be that their host would bring his friends to this particular room, and how stupid of Browning not to notice their remaining garments, including masks, scattered across the floor. Their host most likely didn't care that other guests may be secreted in the room and playing voyeur, or else he knew they were in the wardrobe and wanted to provide some extra entertainment.

Brent, knowing he'd be lucky if Lillian ever spoke to him again after this fiasco, mouthed an apology. Thankfully, she smiled and laid her open palm on his cheek. Christ he loved her. That thought caught him by surprise, and his face no doubt showed his shock, as she raised a brow in silent question. Turning his mouth to nuzzle her palm and give the centre a tiny lick, he gave her a reassuring smile before pasting a neutral expression on his face and dropping his forehead to rest on hers. He was in love with Lady Lillian Armstrong and probably had been for quite some time, though he'd been too absorbed with his growing daughter, and too pig-headed about maintaining their seclusion, that he'd ignored everything else, including why he'd been as excited as a child at Christmas when he anticipated one of Lillian's visits, and why he'd been so wretched after she left.

Uncaring of the antics outside their door, he pulled Lillian into his arms and kissed her the way a man in love kisses his darling. After a momentary hesitation, Lillian's hands slid around his neck and she lifted on her toes to prolong their kisses, slow slides of their mating lips followed by a litany of hungry open-mouthed joinings. Predictably, his erection rose again and prodded her belly, despite his willing it into subsidence. Having her feminine curves molded to his leaner length was incredibly erotic, though he silently cursed himself for starting something he couldn't finish in a wardrobe. When Lillian tilted her hips and rubbed against his erection, his knees almost gave way and his mind grappled for ways he could make love to her in a cupboard. The paneling might collapse and the cupboard would certainly rock on its legs if he took her against a wall, but the ache in his cock was getting harder and harder to ignore and soon he'd be tempted to throw open the door and find another room and damn the consequences.

For himself, he was past caring if he was seen at a courtesan's ball, even stark naked, but he'd never risk Lillian's reputation. The only garment within reach was a silk robe covered in pink and purple cabbage roses and with a frilled neckline but, deciding that beggars couldn't be choosy, he shoved his arms into the sleeves and tied the belt at his waist. Lillian was so amused that she clamped two hands over her mouth to stop giggles from escaping, but he gave a *what-else-can-I-do* shrug and pretended his masculinity remained intact, despite the feminine gilding. Thankfully, Lillian seemed composed, which was in direct contrast to his own distress, emotional and physical, at not managing their time together better.

Counting backwards from a hundred usually calmed him and had taken the edge of the anger and frustration he'd suffered during the last months of his marriage, so he closed his eyes and focused on counting.

One hundred, ninety-nine, ninety-eight, ninety-seven—

'Bloody hell,' Brent yelled.

Lillian had wrapped a hand around his cock, while massaging his balls with her other hand. The wardrobe's door flew open and four faces peered inside.

4

*L*illian screamed.

Brent pushed her firmly behind him and she burrowed behind his broad back and pulled the scarf across her face.

He addressed the occupants of the room as if it was an every day occurrence to hide in a cupboard at an orgy. 'Hello Browning, and Browning's guests,' he said cheerfully. 'Having a nice foursome?'

Before Lillian had dipped her head, she'd glimpsed the faces of their four onlookers. Faces that showed emotions ranging from utter amusement from their host, Browning, curiosity from his male cohort, and easy acceptance from the two half-naked prostitutes. Perhaps for them cupboard sex was normal. The thought made her giggle again and she tried to poke her head out from behind Brent's silk clad bottom to see what Browning would do with them, but Brent reached behind him and pushed her head down again.

'Glad you're enjoying yourself, Mallory.' Browning's

amusement sounded in his voice, and she sensed that he was attempting to shift Brent aside so he could get a look at her face. 'Didn't think naked romps were your cup of tea these days, old boy.' Brent placed a hand on either side of the doorway and planted his feet so their discoverers couldn't push past him. 'Heard you'd become a recluse, Mallory.'

She felt Brent give one of his shrugs, but knew he was faking his careless attitude for her sake. Her neighbor was an extraordinary man and a true gentleman, one of the very few titled men who followed the old rules of honor and the protection of women. Somehow though, he had to save him from any more embarrassment as his mother would double her efforts to see him wed if she heard that Brent had attended an event whose primary purpose was the securing of mistresses. The poor man didn't deserve to suffer for her impulsive actions. If she'd stayed at home and pretended to mourn her repulsive husband, Brent wouldn't have been caught wearing women's clothing.

As if he'd read her mind, Browning said, 'Love that robe, Mallory. The pink roses match the blush on your cheeks perfectly.'

'Stifle it, Browning, and get out of here so my companion and I can redress and leave.'

'Oh, I don't think we'll let you off that easily, will we?'

Lillian heard his companions murmur and chuckle and wondered what Browning had in mind. Whatever he planned, she and Brent were sure to be the focus of his jokes.

Guilt washed over her. 'I'm sorry,' she whispered, hoping Brent would understand. He waggled his fingers behind his back to tell her he understood and she leant her forehead on his back, taking comfort from the fact that she could trust Brent to look after her.

'Come out, come out, who ever you are,' Browning chanted, the two women repeating his chorus over and over. 'Bring your lady out to play with us, Mallory. I have a large bed so the more the merrier.'

'No.' Brent's growled answer told her that he was getting annoyed with Browning and his flippant attitude. 'If you won't leave, Browning, at least hand us our clothes. Most of them are under the bed.'

She heard Browning send his male accomplice to retrieve their belongings, but was shocked when Browning added, 'Lay them on the bed so they can dress there. In exchange for letting you leave, Mallory, we get to watch the two of you dress.'

Brent's sudden movement forward pushed Lillian back- wards and she hit the back wall and landed on her rear with an audible thump. The wardrobe shook as Brent put one bare foot on the floor of the room and grabbed Browning's only garment, his trousers. Lillian clutched the scarf and held it over her face like a shield when Brent drew back his arm and landed a punch between Browning's eyes. Taken by surprise and perhaps drunk on his own punch, Browning fell backwards and landed, arms outstretched, on what was luckily a plush carpet.

'You bastard, Mallory.' Browning's hands were covered in blood where he clutched his nose, while the elder of the two women pushed a piece of linen under his nose to soak up the freely-flowing blood. 'We're leaving and don't try to stop us.' He pointed at the other man. 'Step back and let me collect our clothing, else you'll have a nose to match Browning's.'

Lillian checked that the scarf was in place and wrapped her arms around herself to add extra cover over her breasts as Brent's white shirt was superior quality fabric and likely to be rather transparent. She carefully put her bare feet on the carpeted floor and placed her hand in the middle of Brent's back. He glanced over his shoulder and gave her coverings a quick scrutiny before pulling her forward and tucking her close to his side.

They shuffled towards the bed where he scooped up their belongings and guided her towards the door, taking care to keep his large body and armful of clothes between her and the four guests and thus deprive them of glimpsing her face or coloring. Taking care that her identity was shielded and her reputation untarnished, or at least no more tarnished than when her husband had killed himself over a reckless and foolish bet.

His care of her reminding Lillian why she considered Brent the most honorable man she knew. Very few of the titled men she'd met during her years of attending upper social events had the morals of a true gentleman, and certainly none of Geoffrey's circle stuck to their principles. They acted like sheep and blindly followed whichever leader happened to be in fashion, or had deep pockets, that particular week. Brent had proved the exception, time and again.

When his wife had boasted about her affairs, Brent had visited each of her lovers in turn and threatened them retribution if they discussed his wife, or spoke badly of her. His aim, however, wasn't to stop talk of him being a cuckold, but to stop every gentleman Marion had taken as her lover labeling her a whore or sharing drunken stories about their bedroom romps. No wonder Lillian, his family, his close friends, and his daughter all loved him.

She loved him. She was *in love* with Brent, Earl Mallory, her clever confidant.

Her heart stuttered, her pulse raced, and she stumbled.

Brent tightened his hold on her arm and glanced at her in concern, before guiding her through the doorway and down the corridor. He glanced back to check no one had followed them and then, once again, walked to each door and listened. They needed an empty room, and quickly, so they could redress. The notion of donning her clothes and returning Brent's shirt saddened her as she might never have another chance to see his broad chest or admire his muscled abdomen. She'd used up her meagre supply of seductive tactics when she'd coerced Brent into going upstairs with her. Now she needed and excuse to prolong their night and spend more time together.

'This one,' he said, tugging her inside and depositing his bundle of clothing on a dresser. He turned the key in the lock and wedged a chair under the handle in case Browning decided to search for them and use his master key again. With a heavy sigh he picked up her chemise and gown and handed them to her.

'My corset,' she said, but he shook his head and bent to tug on his trousers.

'No time, besides, I'm taking you straight home.'

She gave him a forlorn look. 'And if I don't want to go home?'

He fastened the last button on his trousers and stood in front of her, running a hand through his already tousled hair. 'Lillian, this isn't how I wanted the evening to end either, but we can't risk lingering here now. Browning's not a bad sort but once he's in his cups, he might mention that I've been here, and with a mystery companion. I'd rather not stay in case his friends decide to probe further and, hopefully, by morning they'll be too busy nursing their sore heads to inquire about my new love.' He turned his back. 'Put on your chemise and then I'll help with your gown.'

Lillian pulled his shirt over her head and then held it her nose. The fabric smelled like him, earthy and male, and she hated having to hand it over. She'd rather keep it as a reminder of how close she'd been to his naked chest, in case she never sighted it again.

She pushed it into his hand. 'Here,' she said, unable to keep the snarl out of her voice.

'Lillian, don't be angry,' he said, still not looking at her. 'I'm sorry. So very sorry. I wanted to...'

She laid her hand on his back and closed her eyes. His skin felt hot and she had a sudden urge to lick, to soothe, and to hold on tight and not let go, yet delaying was imprudent and Brent would fret until he'd removed them both from here. 'What did you want, Brent. Tell me.'

His chest heaved under her palm and a shiver rippled down his spine. "Everything. I wanted to explore every curve and crevice of you body. I wanted to suck your pretty nipples until wiggled and writhed and climaxed and then I was going to slide deep inside you and fuck you until dawn. Take you a dozen different ways.'

She gasped, dropped her forehead to his back, and slid her arms around his waist. He leaned back into her embrace. 'I wanted that too.' She kissed the bare skin between his shoulder blades. 'I still want that, all of it.'

'It will be impossible with you living in the duke's house.'

'Brent, please, I need you. Please tell me we can tray again, somewhere else, by ourselves.'

He covered her hands with his and dropped his head back against hers. 'We'll have to work something out because, Lillian, now that I've kissed you and touched you, I won't let you go. I can't.' He shrugged into his shirt and turned to help her dress in her gown. 'Damnation. No shoes.'

She smiled, trying to lighten the mood. 'Well, I've always wanted to be Cinderella running barefoot from the ball.'

5

*B*rent groaned, slid his hands through Lillian's hanging hair, and kissed her, softly and sweetly. 'You're amazing. I've never met anyone as sweet, yet confident, as you, Lillian.'

'Huh, it's easier to act with confidence and experience when noon knows that I'm Lady Armstrong, widow of a horrible man and dutiful daughter to an over-bearing duke.'

'I know how hard it's been for you and I'd give anything to shoulder some of your burdens and lighten your spirits.'

'Oh, Brent. The only reason I've survived the torment and humiliation of being a disgraced widow is because you wrote to me, every week. Your letters gave me hope that the debates about how Geoffrey died, and why, would eventually lessen and that I simply had to wait until a bigger scandal pushed me off the front page of the gossip rags.' She clasped his cheeks and drew his head down for a kiss. 'You're the reason I'm here.'

'Me? If I'd known about this little adventure of yours, I'd have...' His shoulders sagged. 'I don't know what I'd have done.'

She laughed. 'You'd have done the honorable thing and found a way to stop me, wouldn't you?'

'Well, yes, of course.' He frowned. 'I hate the idea of you being in peril. Of ever being in a situation where someone could hurt you, especially if I'm not there.' He heaved a sigh. 'Thank the heavens that Michael goaded me into coming with him, or one of these rogues might have loaded you with punch and brought you to one of these bedrooms.' He waved his hand to indicate the row of bedchambers on this level of the house.

Lillian threw back her head and laughed.

He shook his head. 'Sweetheart, this isn't a laughing matter. Drunken men, even so-called men of honor, will try any trick to lure a gorgeous woman into bed.'

'Maggie warned me about the drunkenness and we planned how to tip our champagne and punch into the potted plants. My reason for coming wasn't to be dragged into a dark corner by an oaf, but to indulge in a little risqué conversation. Be flattered by admirers who felt free to shower me with compliments instead of discussing the weather, none of which is allowed to happen normally.' She patted his cheek. 'No man, except one I love, would have led me to a bedroom. With you, I was more than willing.'

'Are you saying that --' The door rattled and the knob turned as someone tried to gain entry. He put a finger to Lillian's mouth, silently urging her to remain silent. 'Go away,' he yelled. 'This room is occupied.' Muffled voices and shuffling feet had them holding their breath but after a few tense seconds a woman tittered and hurried footsteps told them the couple have moved along the corridor.

'Hurry, Lillian. We have to leave.'

He tucked in his shirt, helped Lillian tidy her appearance, and bundled her hair under the scarf. Satisfied that

she was as disguised as possible, he put his ear to the door
and listened. Hearing no sounds, he moved the dresser and
turned the key. Keeping Lillian behind him, he eased the
door open and stepped into the corridor.

'Stay beside me and no matter who we encounter, don't
speak.'

'But I need to tell Maggie where I am.'

He groaned. 'All right but I'll look for her and you'll stay
out of sight.'

She nodded and they hurried down the staircase, stopping twice to pull Lillian into an embrace and shield her
face when two couples raced, hand in hand, up the stairs.
His nerves were stretched to breaking by the time they re-
entered the ballroom, so he focused on finding a hiding
place for Lillian while he located Maggie and urged her to
leave with them. However, Lillian would leave in his
carriage and not Maggie's, and he'd brook no arguments.
Some of his anger was directed towards Maggie, who'd
stupidly encouraged Lillian to take unacceptable risks. The
inequality of rules for the upper ten thousand of Britain
meant that men pleased themselves in where they went and
with whom, but women never had the same freedom or
opportunities so he understood that both women yearned
for an evening or two where they could interact with men
on a somewhat equal footing.

But in Brent's mind, their need to escape the confines of
widowhood didn't justify the risks they'd taken and he was
certain he and Lillian would argue about this for a long
time. Too bad, because he'd never accept a situation that
threatened her well-being or her security. Pulling aside the
heavy curtains covering a window niche, he guided Lillian
onto the bench seat and instructed her to stay hidden and
stay silent. He gave her a brief peck on the lips and stiffened

his spine, girding himself to re-enter the fray in the hot and crowded ballroom.

Thirty minutes later, he'd informed Michael he was leaving, and with whom, and had found Maggie. Irritated beyond bearing, he took no time in leading her aside and updating her on the situation. 'We're leaving, all of us. Lillian's waiting.'

Maggie opened her mouth to say something but he cut her off. 'No arguments. I'm out of patience with Browning and all of this.' He waved his hand at the milling men and women and the high-pitched laughs that now grated on his nerves. Maggie obviously grasped his seriousness because she simply nodded, ensured that her mask was firmly in place, and walked directly towards the entrance.

'Fetch Lillian and I'll meet you at my carriage.'

'We'll see you on your way home, wherever that may be, but I will escort Lillian to her house.'

Maggie smiled and raised a brow. 'To her house, or to yours?'

Brent stiffened. 'That's none of your business.'

She laughed. 'I think that answers my question, and I'm pleased. Glad that lovely Lillian finally gets her night with the man of her dreams.'

'Me-e-e. Man of her dreams?' She'd flustered him, and she knew it.

She laughed again and waved him away. 'Go. Fetch Lillian.'

As he hurried away, he shook his head, certain he'd never understand the thinking of women. Even Lillian's ideas and comments often surprised him, yet more times than not he put her suggestions into practice, especially farm improvements.

Twenty minutes later, Brent stood with Lillian as

Maggie's footman helped her into a plain black carriage. "Good night,' Lillian said, hugging her friend. 'And thank you for a wonderful experience.'

Brent groaned. 'An experience never to be repeated. Agreed?' Maggie laughed again and waved to them through the window, while Lillian nodded but stayed silent. He put his hands on his hips and asked again, 'Do you agree?'

"Yes, my lord,' Lillian agreed with blatantly false humility.

Behind him, Brent heard Michael chuckle. He swung to face him. 'Why are you listening to private conversations and what were you and Maggie talking about when we came outside?'

To his annoyance, Michael glanced at Lillian before giving a nonchalant shrug which only helped convince Brent that his friend was hiding something. But what?

'Now that I think about it, you seemed rather familiar with Maggie. Do you know who she is?'

Michael shrugged again. 'Perhaps.'

Brent turned towards Lillian. "Is Maggie her real name?'

'Perhaps,' she said with the same shrug Michael had given, and a wide grin.

'Ha, ha.' He pointed between Michael and Lillian. 'You two are very funny.' He glared at Michael. 'We'll continue this discussion tomorrow. Now, do you want to ride with us?'

'If you don't mind, though I won't come between you lovebirds for too long. I've made arrangements to spend the night not far from here.'

'Who do you know in this area?' Brent closed the carriage door behind Michael and sat opposite him, and beside Lillian. When the driver started the horses and they left Browning's large house behind, a heavy weight lifted from his shoulders. He'd never forget the lurch of his stomach and the stutter of his heart when he'd realized Lillian was in that ballroom surrounded by leering gentlemen who'd been drinking steadily for hours. Not caring that Michael watched them with eagle eyes, he put his arm around Lillian's shoulder and pulled her head to his shoulders. Her eyes closed and she relaxed into his side, allowing him to suck in his first easy breath for hours.

He frowned at Michael. "You haven't answered my question.'

'A gentleman never reveals his affairs, especially if the lady prefers to be discreet.'

Something about Michael's answer roused his suspicions, but he couldn't decipher that puzzle when his thoughts were centered on Lillian and where he was going to instruct his driver to take them. Taking her home to the duke's house would be simplest, but he still ached for her and longed for a second chance, without Browning or anyone lese to interrupt them.

'For God's sake, Brent. I can hear you thinking from over here. The solution isn't that hard. You're in love with Lillian and have been for a long time. And she loves you...' He raised a questioning brow.

Brent nodded. 'Yes,' he whispered, 'I believe she does.' He smiled. 'After Browning found us in the wardrobe--'

'The wardrobe?' Michael rocked with laughter though he at least tried to muffle it and not wake Lillian. 'Reclusive Lord Mallory and the widow Armstrong caught together in a cupboard?' He slapped his hands on his knees and kept laughing. 'Can't wait to share that bit of news with...'

'With?'

Michael put a finger to his lips and nodded towards Lillian. 'You know I'm happy for you. After all you went through with Marion you, of all people, deserve to find happiness. Are you going to ask her to marry you?'

'I...I don't know. We haven't had time to sort out our feelings, or to discuss what happens next. I need to recover from the shock of Lillian mixing with those...girls.'

'She's not as innocent or untouched as you'd prefer to think, Brent. Not after being married to dastardly Geoffrey.'

'She told me some of it tonight, and I feel guilty that I'd not done more. Helped her somehow.'

'Nothing you could have done, old friend. Husbands are allowed treat their wives however they like and no one can interfere. Not even the duke could have taken her away from her husband.'

'Stupid bloody British laws. Time someone brought it up in parliament and pushed for some reform. Even small reforms. To allow women to leave if their lives are in danger from their husbands.'

'Good idea. I know a peer in a position to do that.'

Brent frowned. 'Who?'

'Michael pointed. 'You, my dense friend. Long past time you came out of seclusion and took up your seat. Think of the good you could do for women like Maggie and Lillian.'

Brent narrowed his eyes at Michael. 'What do you know about Maggie?'

Michael thumped on the carriage roof to signal the driver to stop. He touched a finger to his forehead in a mock salute. 'If you want my advice, you'll tell that lovely lady that you love her.'

Michael leapt from the coach onto the road before a large gateway and Brent squinted into the dark as Michael strode towards the iron gates. Too dark outside for Brent to discern the gold-lettered name on the arch, but tomorrow Michael would have some explaining to do. As the driver whipped up the horses, the carriage rocked and Lillian awoke with a start. Looking out the window she said, 'Oh, Maggie's house,' before subsiding into the seat and dropping back into a sound sleep.

Brent threw his head back against the leather headrest and silently laughed. No wonder Michael was being secretive. At this very moment, he was no doubt sauntering down the driveway to Maggie's house where he'd spend the night in the house owners bed. Maggie was a widow who'd suffered at her husband's hand, but Brent knew nothing else about her except that she was Lillian's friend and his softly-snoring sweetheart was generally an excellent judge of character. Perhaps Michael would also fall in love.

6

The carriage pulled to a jerky stop and Lillian awoke with a start. Brent's arm was wrapped about her, holding her close to his side and his warmth and presence reassured her that she was safe. She turned to see him watching her through hooded lids, looking sleepy and ruffled and...delicious.

She pushed herself upright and looked out. 'Oh, Brent.' She smiled. Oh how she loved this man, and now she'd have to chance to show him how good it could be between them. His servants had left a light burning in his house, ready for his return. She reached up and kissed him. 'Thank you for not taking me to my father's house. Thank you for bringing me to you house instead. Thank you for being my best friend.'

He bent his head and took control, kissing her with a hunger that matched hers. Kissing her as if his life depended on having his lips pressed to hers and their breaths mingling. "Let's go inside. My staff will be asleep and I'll take you home before anyone stirs abroad. No one but the two of us will know that I've had you in my arms all night. Had you all to myself, as I've longed to do for what seems like forever.'

Brent used his key to let them inside and ushered her quickly up the staircase. Though she'd been in his house several times, she'd never before been alone with him and a tremor of anticipation rippled through her body. An entire night to explore his long and lean form, so different to her own, thrilled her and she silently thanked Maggie for pushing her into attending the courtesan's ball. Otherwise, her relationship with Brent might never have had the jolt it needed to push them out of their comfortable friendship and into something a lot more exotic.

Her fingers tingled where his bare hand gripped hers, another first as normally they both wore either thick riding gloves or thin leather ones suitable for visiting. And the image of Brent's deliciously male chest and her first glimpse when he'd removed his shirt would stay in her mind forever. Impatient for another moment pressed against him, she slowed, waited until he'd turned and questioned her with his eyes, she drew his head down for another kiss. That he came willingly and met her lips with his as eagerly as she felt, relieved a nagging thought that she might have trapped him into this assignation. While she wanted this intimacy, wanted him desperately, she wouldn't be able to face him year after year if her doubts and fears lingered.

'Tell me honestly,' she whispered, 'that this is what you truly want. There is still time to change your mind and take me home, before we enter your bedchamber and commit to each other. I couldn't live with the guilt if we were somehow discovered and our affair revealed. If you were you trapped into...into...'

'Marriage?'

'Yes.'

He gently wrapped his long fingers around her face and she felt the callouses that proved him the opposite of an idle peer. His hands displayed his love of the outdoors and his willingness to dive into hard work with his estate laborers as if he'd been born to dig soil and mend walls, rather than ride the estate and survey the work from a distance. Those calloused hands told her that he tended to the things, and people, he loved. She yearned to be one of those he loved because Brent's style of loving was an encompassing, dedicated, and for life.

No half measures, and though her parents loved her, she'd never been the absolute focus of anyone's attention. Perhaps she was gluttonous in her need for him, but she'd never be as self centered in her demands as his first wife had been and she'd never drain him, as Marion had, of the innate liveliness that made Brent special. Yes, she'd wallow in joy of having his single-minded attention on her, but she also adored and treasured Brent and longed to shower him with the marital love he'd been denied.

The sweetness of his kiss weakened her knees and she leaned on him as he murmured in her ear, 'Being married to you, my love, would be a joy, not a burden. And as I intend speaking to the duke tomorrow, or rather today, and asking for your hand in marriage, I wouldn't care if every newspaper in England featured slashed our story across their front pages.' His lips touched hers again, sliding back and forth until her legs trembled and only clutching his sleeves stopped her from collapsing in an emotional mess at his feet. Tears ran down her face and she swiped at them.

"You know my father is likely to kick you to the street, no matter your land and titles, if you tell him the entire story.'

'As any good father should do in protection of his daughter.' He waggled his brows and the wall lights showed his white-toothed grin. 'My shotgun is already loaded and ready for any man who keeps my daughter out all night.'

She chuckled, as he'd intended. 'I'm a widow, yet my father meddles in my affairs as if I'm just out of the schoolroom.'

'Again as it should be. If my daughter is as ravishing as you when she'd older, I'll exhaust myself beating away all her admirers.'

Again she laughed. 'Hard to believe when she has her papa wrapped around her little finger and knows he'll do anything to make her happy.'

He smiled. 'She does have a way of getting what she wants from me, so it's good that she'll have a new mama to teach her some restraint.'

'Hmm, much as I'd adore to be her mama, I've not been asked. Yet.'

When Brent dropped to one knee on the passageway's carpet, she gasped and quickly glanced around to ensure they were still alone, but the house remained silent. 'Brent,' she hissed, trying to pull him to his feet. 'I didn't mean here.'

He shrugged and gave her a *don't-care* look. 'By tomorrow, the servants will know you're to be my wife and my daughter will be shouting the news from every window.' He took her hand and rubbed the bare fingers on her left hand. 'Lillian, love of my life, will you marry me and transform me from a forlorn recluse into the happiest peer in the House of Lords?'

'Oh, Brent, does this mean you're finally going to sit in parliament?'

He nodded. 'Isn't that what you've been urging me to do for the past three years?'

Tears flowed again as she said, 'Yes, yes, yes. You'll be brilliant. Our government needs young men with new ideas

who can shake the stubborn old goats out of their compla-
cency. They need you, Lord Mallory, and others like you.
What about Michael? Can you convince him to follow you
into parliament when his father succumbs?'

Brent threw back his head and laughed. "Only you, my
darling Lillian, would view my going into government as
more important than my proposal of marriage.'

Suddenly aware that she'd skimmed over the first part of
his statement and ignored his position on bent knee on the
floor and jumped to the excitement of him as a parliamen-
tarian, she felt ashamed. Her eyes went wide with guilt. 'I'm
so sorry.' She covered her face with her hands but he pulled
them away. 'Perhaps you should rescind your proposal. I'm
certainly not conservative enough to make a good politi-
cian's wife.'

He kissed the backs of her hands and smiled. 'But you're
the perfect wife for me. And I'd really like your answer
because this floor is rather hard on the knees.'

'Yes, yes, yes, I'd be honored to become your wife, Lord
Mallory.' His sagging shoulders told her how tense he'd
been waiting for her answer, though surely he'd guessed
that she'd cultivated their friendship because she'd been
infatuated with him since they'd been children. Rising to his
feet, Brent slipped off his signet ring and slid it onto the
fourth finger of her left hand. 'I love you, Lillian, and I'll do
everything in my power to make you happy.' She clung to
his neck when they shared kiss after kiss.

Tugging her with him, Brent strode to his room and
opened the door. When she was inside, he locked it and
tested that no one could barge into the room, especially his
daughter. 'Alone at last,' he teased. 'We have few hours left
until we face your father and I intend savoring every
moment.'

Lillian groaned. 'I doubt the duke will be thrilled with any of our news. First, he'll be furious that I snuck out of his house last night without the servants noticing because he's keeping close watch over Candace and her recklessness. Secondly, he might not picture you as the best person to polish my reputation, considering the scandal when you fortified Marion's reputation after her affairs. Such heroism is rarely seen in our circles, and therefore your gallantry was misconstrued. As for having a liberal-minded son-in-law sitting with him in Lords, he'll be more incensed by your radicalism than by you having an illicit affair with his daughter.'

While she'd been speaking, Brent had skillfully turned her and, for a second time, eased her out of her garments.'

'You're rather good at that,' she said over her shoulder.

He chuckled. 'I've had lots of practice recently...' She hissed in a breath and he kissed her bared shoulder. 'But only with a small girl's clothing. You're the only woman I've touched in years.'

'I'm glad,' she said with a huff. 'Oh, dear, I sounded like a green-eyed cat, didn't I?'

'I liked it. A lot. Been a long time since anyone cared enough to feel jealous of who I've been with, and I must admit, I'm feeling rather possessive of you too. The thought of any of those louts putting their hand on you tonight drove me crazy. I knocked over a footman's tray of champagne and banged into at least ten women in my rush to find you.'

'Mmm, I must say, I like your eagerness too. A lot.' She pointed at his clothing. 'Lose those, right now.'

He touched a finger to his forehead. 'Yes, milady. What ever you desire.'

She licked her lips. "What I desire is you, naked, and on that bed.'

He groaned and she watched in awe as his cock swelled and stood upright. She pressed against him, reveling in the feel of his hard length wedged between their bodies, but when his fingers ran through the nest of hair between her legs, her knees threatened to give way again. Scooping her up, Brent strode to his bed and laid her on her back, following her down to lie over her, stretched to his full-length and with his weight resting on his elbows.

'I need to send Maggie a gift. What would she like?'

She pushed at his shoulder and mocked, 'Tut, tut. Not even married and you're lavishing gifts on other women.'

'Only one woman. The one to whom I'll be endlessly indebted. Without Maggie, I might have regarded you from a discreet distance for another four years, because I came with the encumbrance of a daughter and a sordid past marriage.'

'I adore your daughter and my marriage became a more sordid tale than yours, so cease this talking and make love to me. Please.'

He nodded, his expression full of love and his eyes moist, before licking one nipple and twiddling the other. Her back arched and she was lost in a continuation of the lust and longing she'd felt in Browning's house. After licking her second nipple, Brent blew air over them and she shivered. Shivered again when he used one knee to spread her thighs and rubbed himself, hot and engorged, up and down between her wet folds.

She groaned. 'So good, Brent. So very good.'

'We've a long way to go yet, my love.'

She clutched handfuls of his hair as he slid down further and opened his mouth over her mons and sucked, insistently. She screamed his name as the first waves of pleasure hit and ran through her body. Screamed again when he took her clit between sharp teeth and tugged. Screamed and sobbed when he moved up and thrust inside her welcoming channel, withdrawing and plunging in an erotic rhythm that her calling his name over and over, like a series of prayers that praised his actions, yet begged him for release.

'Oh, yes, sweetheart. Let yourself fly. Come for me, my darling.'

When she spasmed again and squeezed him with her inner muscles, he threw back his head and yelled, plunging into her two...three...four times until he jerked and her womb filled with his hot seed. Nothing in her life had ever felt so good, so right. Still inside her, Brent rolled them so she was spread across him and with his arms encasing her trembling body. Their breathing was ragged, as if they'd raced on their horses across his fields and not stopped for rest. Her nose was pressed to his chest and she inhaled his familiar smell of a physically active male. In an instant, her lust stirred and she wriggled her groin against his flaccid penis and giggled like a girl when it twitched and grew.

'Like what you do to me, do you, my temptress?'

She moved her head up and down on his chest to signify her approval. 'Very much so, and I love that I can tempt you because, with Geoffrey, I felt inadequate, especially when he flaunted one mistress after another in my face.'

He put a finger under her chin and forced her to look him in the eye. 'You are the most enticing woman I've ever known and you have the figure of a goddess. In fact, I was about to call out the next supposed gentleman at Browning's who sniffed your hair or peered down your bodice.'

She giggled again. 'Truly?'

'Truly.'

Those were the last words the spoke until the sun's rays through the window glass alerted them to the hour and the need to dress. Before they left the house, Brent pulled her aside and kissed her. Her heart was full to bursting and she took courage from his nonchalant attitude over any prying neighbors and stiffened her spine. Barefoot, her hand in Brent's, and her head held high, Lillian walked to the waiting coach. And when he stole another kiss as he handed into his carriage, Lillian kissed him back. Let the gossips spread their tales, because for the first time in Lillian's life, she felt safe and secure, and above all, loved unconditionally.

7

'How dare you enter my house before I've finished my breakfast and say such things.' The duke's outraged voice shook the walls of the breakfast room and echoed down every corridor, where Brent assumed every member of the duke's staff would be gathered to listen to their news.

Nevertheless, he stepped closer to the duke and his upturned chair and spoke in his normal voice. He refused to cower before the duke and if the servants listened and spread their story all over Mayfair in under an hour, so be it.

He and Lillian were marrying and nothing would stop them, not her growling father or the gossiping peers who delighted in destroying people's reputations and watching their prey scurry away form London to hide. They'd both endured enough gossip and seclusion and today was a new beginning.

A hand in the middle of his back reminded him that Michael stood behind, demonstrating that their family supported each other and were displaying a united public front. Seeing Maggie and Michael waiting outside the duke's house had been a surprise, but when his cousin explained their presence, Brent had been overcome by emotion. Michael and Maggie had expected Brent to present himself before Lillian's father and had decided to stand beside him, as Maggie's father was one of the duke's closest cohorts and she'd know the family all her life. Later, Brent decided, he'd get to the bottom of Maggie's identity and why mystery surrounded her, but for now he was grateful that there were four people in the room in support of a short engagement and, hopefully, their long marriage.

Lillian tucked her arm though Brent's and smiled up at him. 'Papa, Lord Mallory is doing the proper thing by speaking to you, but hear this, we will marry, with or without your permission.'

The duchess pushed back her chair and rushed to hug her daughter and Brent looked down at Lillian and smiled. "You should be pleased, your Grace, that your daughter is so much like you. Strong, intelligent, and loyal.'

The duke's face was red and his fists clenched as he pondered Brent's praise, but when the duchess moved and slid her hand around her husband's elbow and leaned into him, his bluster dissipated. 'Very well, you may court my daughter for six months and if, at that time, I consider you an appropriate husband, you will have my permission to marry.'

'One week,' Brent announced with a smile for everyone in the room. 'I shall procure a special license this morning and Lillian will be married in my local church on Saturday.'

The duke shouted, the duchess patted his arm sooth-ingly, and Lillian's sister raced to embrace her and offer excited congratulations. Beside him, Michael used the hand not holding Maggie's to thump Brent on the back. 'Well done. Expected a bigger battle but you've made your point and robbed the duke of speech, which is a first. Can't wait until he hears your views on law reforms. That's sure to cause a war.' Michael's chuckle was cut off when the duke roared again. 'Law reforms?' He shook his fist at Brent and Michael. 'Over my dead body.'

The duchess spoke and, although her tone was mild, her voice was laced with steel. 'If you don't calm yourself, we'll be laid out in a coffin before the wedding on Saturday. Now, congratulate your daughter and her betrothed and finish your breakfast.'

'Yes, my dear,' the duke muttered, lowering himself into the chair rescued by a smirking footman. He pointed to them. 'Sit down, all of you. Have some tea.' He scowled at Maggie. 'And then you can explain your part in this so I can decide if I need to write to you father and tell him he needs to take better control of his daughter.' He glared at Brent. 'Daughters are the very devil, Mallory, and I hope yours is better behaved than this unruly lot.' He glared at each of his daughters in turn, lingering on Candace who was unable to hide her excitement. 'Give a man gray hairs, they do.'

"My daughter is only six, Your Grace, and yet she seems to bend my entire household to her will with extraordinary ease.'

His Grace snorted, and then took up his cutlery and returned to his meal. Maggie and Michael seated themselves at the table and joined the conversation, while Lillian's sisters talked over the top of one another about their sisters wedding and what gowns they would wear. Brent seized the opportunity to slip outside, urging Lillian with him. Once in the corridor, Lillian took charge and led him to a small room at the very back of the house, locking the door behind them.

They smiled at each other, and then kissed.

'That went far better than I expected,' Brent said. 'You father didn't even send for his gun.'

"I was surprised too, though I think my family has always known how much I admired you and how much I valued your friendship.'

'I love you, Lillian, and I'm sorry that it took me so long to realize how much you meant to me.'

She out a finger to his lips. 'No, you have nothing to apologize for. I'm pleased that we've finally found each other, my love.'

'I promise that I'll do anything to make you happy, Lillian. Anything you want.'

'Anything?'

He nodded, though the look in her eyes worried him a little.

She lifted to her toes and whispered in his ear. 'I want to kneel before you, my darling, and worship your body that way. Will you let me?'

Brent groaned, and then nodded. "But only if I get to kneel before you as well.'

They laughed and kissed and Brent was wondering if he Lillian could be quiet enough to make love in this room, with her family breakfasting not far from them. He slid her gown up and over her knees and then dropped to kneel before her. He inhaled deeply. Oranges and lemons, and sweet Lillian. He parted her nest of hair with his thumbs and then licked up though her folds. Lillian gave a small scream so he knew she was enjoying his ministrations.

The door handle rattled and she screamed again. He popped up from between Lillian's thighs to come face to face with Maggie and Michael, and with Candace poking her head between them. 'Damn master keys,' Brent moaned, but when Lillian laughed aloud and the other joined her, he had no choice but to join their madness. He swung Lillian up into his arms and twirled her around, throwing back his head and laughing until his sides ached.

He slid a smiling Lillian down his body and onto her feet. 'I love you.'

To his amusement, the rest of Lillian's family flooded into the room and surrounded them. Maggie clapped and the others joined in.

'And I love you,' she said as they moved as one to sink into a long kiss.

EXCERPT: FOUR TIMES A VIRGIN

1821, April 1st, Duke of Stirkton's residence, Mayfair, London

"You want me to be your mistress?" The Countess of Dorchester's sculpted brow rose in an exaggerated show of disbelief.

Being the object of someone's ridicule might be a novel experience for Maximus Meacham, Duke of Stirkton, but it wasn't one he cared to repeat, even if the woman laughing at his proposal spoke like a queen and looked like a goddess. Max brushed an imaginary speck from the sleeve of his evening jacket and pretended he couldn't see her half-hearted attempts at smothering her chuckles with her gloved hand.

"And I'm to be at your beck and call for precisely one month?"

He looked up and caught her inspecting him from head to toe. When her gaze lingered around the area of his groin, his muscles contracted, his body heated and his bollocks tightened. He turned away. If the Countess knew that her one lingering appraisal of his manly assets could turn a cold and controlled duke into a lustful male, he'd lose control of their situation and his years of planning would amount to nothing.

The Countess would take what she'd come for: his grandfather's lists, and his fantasy of having her as his lover —even for four weeks—would evaporate faster than his dreams of a happier new day had, when his grandfather had thrown open his bedroom door each morning and berated him for failing to arise and greet the dawn.

He glanced sideways. His breath seized and he mentally revised his description of her beauty. With porcelain skin, auburn curls, and emerald eyes that hinted at a Scottish lineage, the Countess had grown into one of the most stunning women he'd ever laid eyes on. Max's comparison was based on intimate knowledge of some of the most exquisite women in England. Not even his imagination had done her justice, and he'd spent many long nights picturing how she'd look when, or if, they ever found her again. Wondering if she'd aged gracefully, or more importantly, if she'd lived disgracefully after he and his grandfather had turned her young girl's life on its head? Though his fantasy woman had carried a girlish countenance and had worn significantly less clothing than this girl who captured his attention in an ill-lit room at a country inn.

He risked another look at his unexpected visitor. This lady wore a gown that wrapped her body as closely as a lover's arms, and he knew from the pile of bills he paid to whichever modiste that month's mistress preferred that the Countess's outfit would have cost a pretty penny.

While he snatched quick and gentlemanly looks at the Countess's face and dress style, she continued her own perusal. Her study of him and his entire body was so slow and intense that he felt his skin heat and prickle.

As the Duke of Stirkton, he was well accustomed to being watched. Young pups copied his dress style. Toad-eaters mimicked his behavior in futile attempts to ingratiate themselves into his life. Conservative groups applauded his somber public behavior, while cartoonists ridiculed his straight-laced demeanor and suggested he take a mistress. Or two.

Whichever way people viewed him, no one had dared ridicule him to his face. Until this evening. The Countess had side-stepped his butler and marched into his drawing room as if an unannounced call upon an unmarried duke was something she did regularly. Max had informed her, in great detail, of the extensive search he and his cousin had undertaken to locate her and the other women. She'd huffed and rolled her eyes. Normally, his month-about-mistresses gleefully accepted his proposal because sharing a duke's bed for a month would set them up for the rest of their lives. Apart from the financial benefits, he was a generous lover. One benefit of his abnormal upbringing had been an early and full education into what women wanted in a bed partner. Until the Countess had laughed at him, he'd never had reason to doubt his sexual prowess. In the brief time she'd been in his house, she'd challenged several of his beliefs.

"It's the ideal solution." And something he needed. "I will help you search my grandfather's boxes by day and, in exchange, you'll make yourself available to me in the evenings." Max waited, unsure what to expect. An odd situation for a man who prided himself on reading adversaries as easily as he tallied the accounts.

"Ah, I understand." She nodded, and the crimson curls artlessly dangling from the knot on her crown bounced around her shoulders and settled on the bare flesh exposed above the fashionable square-cut of her evening gown. "You're jesting."

His body's acute, and for recent times, abnormal physical response, distracted him. He envied those curls and their freedom to touch her lightly-tanned skin. "I never jest."

"You're seriously asking me to play your courtesan for this month?" She walked around him, tiny circling steps meant to disconcert him. "Me?" She threw her arms wide in a theatrical gesture. "Act like a common cyprian? A demimondaine squeezed in between business meetings. Or, in our case, between boxes of files." She waited for his nod. "But why?"

"Why not?" Max's compulsion to provoke this woman, the girl selected for him in Dorchester and whose name had eluded him for eight long years, was childish. Ridiculous behavior for a man taught from birth that Meachams exhibited the same haughty arrogance as the Royal Family, no matter the circumstances. Yet he'd tried to discompose the Countess from the moment she'd arrived and faced him, toe to toe. He glanced at the ornate clock on his mantle. Twenty minutes had passed in a flash. He feared blinking in case the erstwhile Lady Carina Woods vanished as swiftly as she had from the Dorchester inn, swept away in an elegant but discreetly blackened carriage.

Now, the widowed Countess looked cool, calm and more magnificent than any of his dream manifestations. Even while looking at him as though he was an escapee from Bedlam.

"What you're proposing is ludicrous."

"To the contrary, my proposal is serious, sane, and expedient." Though he knew his idea sounded insane when voiced aloud. "Before I agree to your searching through my grandfather's documents, I need your agreement to my terms."

He was a fool, an obsessed idiot who'd been thrown into confusion at her unannounced arrival and hadn't taken his usual time to prepare his argument. The moment she'd set foot in his house, a life-time of training had been forgotten as he'd scrambled for ways to secure her attention and her promise. By habit, he glanced towards the portrait holding pride of place on the long wall. He shivered when his grandfather's eyes, blue and as cold as arctic ice chips, stared back at him. The late Duke had controlled every step of Max's growing years and had taught him, with the aid of his riding crop, rules that must be followed so the family name and reputation would continue, unsullied by weakness or doubt.

Max's first sexual experience had been on his fourteenth birthday, another lesson, with the woman selected, instructed and paid for by his grandfather. Max's tutelage in ducal dominance in the bedroom had been scheduled on his calendar alongside accounting lessons, because Augustus had believed that regular sex was a messy yet necessary part of a duke's life in the same way food ensured a man's physical wellbeing. Max was trained to control his sexual responses, harden his heart and view a woman's body as a means to an end, while his companions were employed on a rotating monthly basis. If their month passed with no complications, each courtesan was well compensated. Women were to be scrutinized for cleanliness and sensuality with the same objectivity a duke was expected to give to the side of mutton or slab of beef served by his chef each night. But after years of searching for this particular woman, Max feared that adhering to those rigid Meacham rules would be as impossible as disobeying Augustus had been when he was a child.

"A proposal? You issued a ducal command." The disappointment in the Countess's statement drew his gaze, and his thoughts, back to her. "And you believed I'd accept as if I was a well-trained whore. You may be accustomed to women rushing to do your bidding, but I'll never again be ordered about by a man."

EXCERPT LOVING LADY KATHARINE

I lived in Vanuatu, previously the New Hebrides, in the South Pacific for nine years and loved the island life and its fascinating history. Kelly's Justice is set in contemporary Vanuatu and Loving Lady Katharine in historic Vanuatu. I hope you enjoy reading both versions of Vanuatu.

1860 New Hebrides, Pacific Ocean.

At first, all Lord Alexander St. John had gleaned was that Lady Katharine Montgomery was the young widow of a British Lord and yet she now ran, efficiently and unobtrusively, her father's extensive businesses in the largest town in the New Hebrides, a large group of islands in the South Pacific. Her father, a cruel Scots man estranged from his family, beat her whenever he was drunk or whenever something reminded him of their forced and hasty departure from London.

But less than twenty four hours ago, Robert McLeish, Katie's father, had been laid to rest in the small burial ground beside the open-sided erection that passed for a church. Father Bryan struggled to speak complementary words of the man as the coffin was lowered into the ground, yet Katie stood dry eyed, her only feelings being those of profound relief. She was finally free.

Robert McLeish, with his usual arrogant disregard for the native's warnings, had pushed his horse through dense undergrowth on his distant plantation and a wild boar had startled his horse into throwing him, where after he had sustained repeated attacks from the monstrous animal.

People had moved around her at the house, offering tea and sympathy, mainly speaking pathetic lies of what a good man her father had been. No one believed them, least of all his only daughter. The European population on the island was small so Katharine's situation with her father had been well understood although never spoken of as in some way they all depended on their trade business to supply goods to the town. MacLeish's temper was legendary and none had dared to interfere.

'Katharine, please let us know if we can help in any way.'

'Lady Katharine, will you now be returning to England?'

She stared at the speaker intently before replying. 'I have nothing to return to.'

'It is impossible for you to remain alone in the house now. Certainly not fitting for a lady.'

Now she almost laughed, her thoughts mixed with a touch of hysteria. If they only knew. This hell hole was fitting for a woman like her.

Katie stifled rising feelings of frustration and anger with their questions to mingle with her guests, finding it easier to fix her face into her normal unemotional mask and agree with their lies about her father rather than acknowledge the unspoken truth.

Finally the house emptied, except for Alexander. She'd been polite, formal and firm at her first attempt to get him to leave, to leave her alone with her thoughts, but he insisted on staying, worried about her state of mind. After plying her with three whiskies from her father's best bottle, a bottle she'd never been allowed lay a finger on before, he drew her unresistingly to the large bamboo settee on the front verandah.

'Sit, Katie! Rest a while. You're exhausted.'

She stared at him with unseeing eyes. He sat close to her, his thigh almost touching hers through the skirts of her black mourning dress. This dress, like everything else he'd seen her wear, was practically threadbare and hopelessly out of fashion but here on her beloved island, Katie wouldn't have given such frivolous things a thought.

'I know you didn't like your father...'

Expressing the first real emotion he'd seen all day she yelled, 'Like? I despised him. My father was a tyrant just like...'

His stroked her arm. 'Like your husband?'

She shot off the settee, gaping at him. Unused to alcohol, she rocked on her feet but when he reached out to steady her, she jumped backwards. 'No, don't touch me. What do you know about my...my husband? No one knows. Only my father and he's dead. He's dead and I'm happy! Do you hear me, happy!' The last came out as as a shout and she looked skyward, as if expecting to be struck down. Though if she wanted her father to hear, she should have shouted at the floor because a man as evil as her father would be looking up, not down.

Watching closely to make sure she didn't hurt herself, he gave her the space she obviously needed to be able to tell her story. And even then, he didn't think she would have unburdened her hidden story of shame and grief if she hadn't been slightly inebriated. Her arms wrapped her waist in a defensive manner and he tried to picture her life. Being under the control of two men who'd alternatively ignored and then abused her must have been a living nightmare.

Keeping his words soft, he'd encouraged her to share with him. 'Katie, I know your father beat you but I never understood 'why.'

Katie clutched the bamboo railing wrapping the verandah. This house had been her father's pride and joy. 'My father loved to stand here and look down on the town and the docks. High enough to spit on the world down below. High enough for him to feel superior to everyone.' Flinging her arms wide, she nearly toppled over the balcony but waved away his aid.

This was where Katie had first met Alex, less than two months earlier, and from that moment her mind had constantly drifted to him, hoping his ship would return soon. Her father's pompous voice had been disgustingly boastful as he announced one morning, 'I am bringing a guest for dinner tonight. Alexander St.John. Soon to be the Duke of St John as I have heard that his father's health is failing quickly. Alexander will inherit the title, the properties and ships that go with it.'

His sneering glance raked Katie's thin figure. 'It's a pity you are so ordinary or I may have entertained the thought of giving you to him as an incentive to trade, but unfortunately he has been betrothed from birth to some chit in England.' Katie had inwardly flinched at the insult from her father, but she schooled herself to not give him the satisfaction of seeing her mortification.

'Be sure to instruct the cook to prepare an excellent dinner. Mr. St. John will one day be a man of great importance. Work in the back room at the warehouse today but return to the house in good time to ensure everything is in place for dinner. We will be at the house at six o'clock. I expect everything to be perfect because if you embarrass me in any way, you know the consequences.'

Katie knew exactly how many lashings her father would deal out for each imaginary sin she committed. Her father enjoyed inflicting pain and even the mildest protest would see him double the lashings. She depended on the healing lotions Tong Lee prepared to prevent further scarring on her back.

The menu had been perfect, her father drooling with greed at the memory of the lucrative business deal he had just concluded with his guest. Conversation had been intelligent and enjoyable and for the first time in many years, Katharine was able to relax in the company of a well bred man. For the first time in her twenty six years, she felt a flutter in her stomach, her body heating as she met his direct, appraising glance. Something flashed between them. Something she had no knowledge of previously and didn't know how to deal with now.

Then the unthinkable had happened. Alex had spoken directly to her. Simply addressed a question towards her across the dinner table, unleashing a chain of events.

'Lady Katharine, your father tells me you attend to his accounts in the warehouse. I am impressed with your talents. Do you enjoy working there?'

Even as she raised her eyes to answer, a fleeting smile on her lips, her father burst in with his malicious evil. 'Of course she doesn't enjoy it. Who would enjoy living in this God forsaken hell hole, but it is because of her...Lady Katharine...that we are both forced to endure here. She had it made in London, a Lady married to a Lord of the realm with a powerful and influential family. All she had to do was lie in the marriage bed and open her legs to produce an heir.

But would she do it? No! She was too good for that, too above herself, thinking she was better than any of his family just because she is educated, reads books.'

Katharine gasped, her face burning and her mortification complete as she staggered out of her chair, knocking it over in her haste but bravely facing her father. 'You forget!' Her voice was reaching hysteria, yet she stood her ground firmly. 'It was your greed that forced me into that situation. You gave me to that man knowing what he was. What he expected.'

Her father's swift answer was an open handed slap across her face that knocked her sideways. Without looking their shocked guest in the eye, Katharine covered her reddened face, regained her footing and turned to escape the room. Alexander sprang to his feet, trying to capture her arm before she fled. 'Lady Katharine...' But she lifted her skirts and flew out the door and into the garden.

Alexander was outraged on Katharine's behalf. In his experience women were to be protected. 'Mr. McLeish! I hardly think this is suitable dinner table conversation. She is your daughter.'

'Daughter! Daughter!' He was choking on the words, drunk on wine and whiskey as he flung back his own chair, slamming his fist on the table and spewing his rage. 'She is no daughter of mine. She disgraced me. I now have to live my life here.' He threw his arm wide to indicate the small cluster of houses grouped below the hill where his house stood. 'This nowhere!' A malicious gleam sprang into his bloodshot eyes. 'But soon I will be rich. Rich enough to return to London. Then my stupid daughter, the Honorable Lady Katharine, can stay here. She can repay me by continuing to run my business interests here.'

Alexander had been even more shocked. 'You can't be

serious! The port is full of rough seaman and unscrupulous men. You can't mean to leave your daughter here by herself, with no one to protect her?'

'Protect her? Protect her from what? You've seen her. No man would want her. I could never imagine why Lord Percival married her in the first place until I understood the true situation later. She should have been grateful... despite what he was.'

Alexander's question was deceptively quietly spoken. 'What he was?'

Under the weather with drink, Robert let his tongue run away with him for a few minutes.

'Well who would have guessed what persuasion he was? How could I have known?' His look was sly, almost evil, and Alexander knew without doubt that this man had known exactly the situation he had sent his daughter into. 'Anyway, it should have made no difference to Katharine. She was his wife regardless and should have done her duty. If she had, the truth would have stayed hidden. That...that... other man's wife would never have found out. Never have found them together and taken a gun to them.'

Belatedly recalling who he was talking to, another peer of the realm, Robert pulled himself together. 'Never mind that now. How about another shot of my fine whiskey?'

Nearly choking on rising bile, Alex forced himself to exit politely. 'I thank you sir, but as I sail on the first tide tomorrow, I will bid you goodnight.'

He desperately wanted to race to the gardens and search for Katharine. To assure himself she was all right, but he couldn't afford to be anything but detached with her father. He'd heard the stories of his repeated cruelty. Yet if he remained in the same room as that vile man for another minute, there was no saying that his rage could be contained and the only thing that held him back was worry.

He strode down the flare lit path away from the house until out of sight and then turned into the gardens to search. When a soundless shadow stepped out of the bushes in front of him, he jumped. Tong Lee put a finger to his lips in a gesture of silence and beckoned Alex to follow. Wordlessly, they descended to the small cove where Tong Lee simply stopped and pointed. Huddled on the beach, Alex could make out a small figure sitting in misery and staring fixedly out to the ocean. Not wanting to scare her, he cleared his throat softly to announce his approach... but still she started in fright and fear.

'It is only I, Alexander. Please do not fear me. I didn't wish to alarm you but I needed to be assured of your well being before I left.'

'If my father knows you have spoken to me, he'll... he'll...'

Shuddering at the stories of the man's harsh treatment of his daughter and miserable at the thought that he had been the hapless cause of yet another beating for her, sickness overwhelmed him. While he had fought often with his own father over the years, one of the main reasons he'd gladly left England behind, his father would never inflict physical pain on either he or his three sisters.

He cleared his throat and struggled to settle his agitation before speaking. 'He'll what? Beat you? I am so sorry. I didn't mean to cause you any more distress. Is there any way I can help?'

The look in her eyes as she now fully stared at him was a picture of helplessness and hopelessness. 'There is nothing anyone can do for me. Please leave now before he finds you here or it will be worse for me tomorrow.'

Without moving, he raised his face heavenwards as he searched urgently for an answer, any answer. 'I sail with the morning tide, but I return in a month. May I have your permission to search you out privately then, away from your father? I wish I could help. I wish I knew how.

Please know that I will think of little else during the next month, but you. Lady Katharine, I deeply regret the suffering I have caused you.'

Receiving no reply, he gave a little bow, turning to walk away. Finally the moonlight lit her face with the ghost of a smile as she whispered. 'Katie. Call me Katie. My friends do.'

He halted. Turned to her. Gently, he reached out to touch one finger to her swollen cheek. 'Thank you Katie. My friends call me Alex. Keep well until I will see you next. Watch for me at the next full moon. Perhaps we could ride together.'

She didn't reply, yet as he walked mutely along the sand to the harbor he heard the faintest of whispers, 'Farewell Alex.' The finality in it wrenched at him. She never expected to see him again. In her whole life, she had never been able to depend on any man and she fully expected the same from him. Guilt washed over him at the thought that he may have unwittingly caused such torment in any other woman in his past life. Never again would he be casual with the feelings of women he knew. All women were treasures and deserved to be treated as such.

Tong Lee fell in silently beside him to match his stride. He was becoming accustomed to the Chinaman's shadowy presences and spoke quietly to him. 'Will she be safe? Will he beat her?'

'Yes, he will beat her tomorrow when he wakes and his head is sore. But after I will take care of her as I always do.'

Alex reached into his pocket and pulled out ten gold coins. 'Use these to buy what you need to look after her.'

Tong Lee merely averted his eyes from the money and bowed. 'I will care for her as I always have. As if she is my own daughter.'

Alex insistently pressed the money into his hand and closed his fingers around the coins. 'Please! Keep her safe until I return.'

The ship's sailing kept him too busy to reflect on what had happened but eventually they were under sail and he collapsed onto his bunk. He felt like a miserable coward, leaving a woman with that monster of a father. But what could he do? He had a betrothed awaiting him in England. A girl he hadn't seen for five years yet his family had committed him. To her and to the shipping business. If he stepped in to save Lady Katharine and lost the business, he may well cause the down fall of his entire family. Could he risk it. Two sisters in London depended on his money to give them a season to find a suitable match. Could he jeopardize it all. Risk the scandal by rescuing Katie from her father. But once he had rescued her, what then? What could he possibly do for her.

And so it was that around the next full moon, Katie's eyes drifted continually to the horizon, scouring every boat that arrived, hoping to glimpse Alex's arrival. Her back had healed once again from her father's lashing but this time a new hope blossomed inside her. Not that she allowed her expectations to climb very high. The past had taught her caution.

ABOUT THE AUTHOR

Tag Line - Making history fun, one year at a time.

I now live in a sunny part of Australia after spending many years in developing countries in the South Pacific. I love traveling, anywhere and everywhere, meeting crazy characters, and visiting the Australian outback.

My sexy heroes and feisty heroines challenge tradition, and though they might live a privileged life, they also understand the seamier parts of life.

I can be found in many Facebook groups talking about books and history and am always busy on Twitter, Instagram, and my personal favorite, Pinterest.

To learn more about Suzi Love and my new releases, join my newsletter at my suzilove.com. I am on Instagram and Goodreads and have lots of Pinterest Boards as suziloveoz . And please join my Facebook Group, Suzi Love's Lovelies, to keep up with my news on books and history.

Please visit my WEBSITE

Email me: suzi@suzilove.com

BOOKS BY SUZI LOVE

Fiction By Suzi Love

Embracing Scandal Book 1 Scandalous Siblings Series

Scenting Scandal Book 2 Scandalous Siblings Series

December Scandal Book 3 Scandalous Siblings Series

The Viscount's Pleasure House Book 1 Irresistible Aristocrats

Four Times A Virgin Book 2 Irresistible Aristocrats

Pleasure House Ball Book 3 Irresistible Aristocrats

Petunia and the Pearl Diver Book 4 Irresistible Aristocrats

Loving Lady Katharine Book 5 Irresistible Aristocrats

Love After Waterloo

Kelly's Justice

Outback Arrival

Old Sydney Town

Non-Fiction By Suzi Love

History Of Christmases Past Book 1 History Events

Easter In Images Book 2 History Events

History of Valentine's Day

Regency Overview Book 1 Regency Life Series

Young Gentleman's Day Book 2 Regency Life Series

Older Gentleman's Day Book 3 Regency Life Series

Young Lady's Day Book 4 Regency Life Series

Older Lady's Day Book 5 Regency Life Series

Self Publishing: Absolute Beginners Guide.

HISTORY NOTES SERIES

Here are some of the many titles in this Non-Fiction History Series.

Coming Soon:-
History Notes Underwear
History Notes Grand Tour
History Notes Mail Deliveries
History Notes Peerage
History Notes Food
History Notes Carriages
History Notes Money
History Notes Sewing
History Notes Hats
History Notes Mourning
History Notes Furniture
History Notes Shoes
History Notes Trades
History Notes Clubs
History Notes Fans
History Notes Sports
Historic London
Overview
Bridges
Hospitals
Churches
Famous

REVIEWS

Reviews are like gold to authors. I would appreciate it if you could leave a review, good or bad, for this book at any book retailer.

And don't forget, to get insider news about my book releases, any discounted books or contests that I am a part of, you should sign up for my newsletter. I promise you will only ever hear from me when I have exciting news, about me or my other author friends. www.suzilove.com

You can send me an email : suzi@suzilove.com.

Or send a letter : Suzi Love, 258/ 52 University Way, Sippy Downs, Queensland, 4556, Australia.

www.ingramcontent.com/pod-product-compliance
Lightning Source LLC
Chambersburg PA
CBHW072011170626
46813CB00005B/2104